Christmas in Virginia

A Collection of Holiday Stories

Narielle Living

Lavender Press
An imprint of Blue Fortune Enterprises LLC

Cactus Mystery Press Titles by Narielle Living

Brewster Square Series Cozy Mysteries:

Madness in Brewster Square
Birding in Brewster Square

Paranormal Mysteries:

Signs of the South
Revenge of the Past
Children of the Tribe

CHRISTMAS IN VIRGINIA
Copyright © 2018 by Narielle Living.

This book is a work of fiction. Names, characters, businesses, organizations, places, events and incidents either are the product of the author's imagination or are used fictitiously. Any resemblance to actual persons, living or dead, events, or locales is entirely coincidental.

For information contact :
Blue Fortune Enterprises, LLC
Lavender Press
P.O. Box 554
Yorktown, VA 23690
http://blue-fortune.com

ISBN: 978-1-948979-14-6

First Edition: December 2018

DEDICATION

To my family: past, present and future
May the love that shines throughout the holiday season continue
to be present for all. Thank you for giving me a strong foundation,
for providing me with positive memories, and for giving me reason
to believe that the magic will continue.

Table of Contents

Introduction

Welcome to *Christmas in Virginia*, a series of short holiday stories that take place in and around Hampton Roads, Virginia. I love reading and writing stories about the holiday season because there is such a feeling of possibility in the air, a sense that anything can happen at any time.

The first three tales in this book are centered around Percy, a unique being who has been sent to help others during times of difficulty. Percy's love is evident in all that he does, and he works hard to bring the true spirit of the season to those who need it most.

The fourth story in this book, *A Different Kind of Christmas*, is set in a future world. I had once been challenged to write a fantasy holiday story, and this is the result.

And the final story, *Lucky Christmas*, has characters from one of my books, *Revenge of the Past*. This is a stand-alone story, and although it's not necessary to read *Revenge of the Past* you do get a deeper look at two very special people: Nick and Kylie.

I hope you enjoy reading this as much as I enjoyed writing it. And to all readers everywhere, I wish you peace and love during not only the holiday season but throughout the year.

Marielle Living

A Family for Christmas

CHAPTER ONE

SHE CAUGHT THE DARK SHAPE out of the corner of her eye, while the scrutiny of someone burned on her back. Every now and then a soft exhale came from behind her. Zoe knew without question that she was being followed.

The busy department store boasted an array of glittering Christmas decorations with piped-in music reminding shoppers to be merry. Halloween was barely a memory, but the holiday smell of cinnamon and evergreens wafted through the space. With temperatures still hovering in the seventies, it was holiday time in Virginia.

Through the haze of forced holiday cheer, Zoe saw her two foot tall stalker playing peek-a-boo from inside the skirt rack in the juniors department.

"Are you following me?" Zoe demanded.

A bright, dimpled smile and a short giggle answered her. Her young shadow wasn't even old enough to talk.

Zoe scanned the store, trying to find the child's parents. Nobody was paying attention to the little girl, but maybe her family was busy shopping.

"Where's your mommy, honey?"

Somber eyes looked up at Zoe, answering with a silent gaze.

"No? Does that mean you don't know where they are? Are you lost?" Zoe's heart melted at the sight of this adorable little girl standing in the misses' clothes rack. Large hazel eyes stared up from a round face framed by blonde curls.

"Why don't you come on out of there, your parents might be looking for you." Zoe held her hand out to the child, who immediately ran to her and reached out, wordlessly asking to be picked up. Without hesitation, Zoe lifted the child into her arms.

"Okay, kiddo, I know you didn't drive here by yourself. Let's see if we can find who you belong to."

Zoe walked through the store with the child, hoping someone would spot them and come running over. "Let me know when you see someone from your family. I'm sure they're frantic by now." As they wandered, the little girl let loose with a stream of babble. It was impossible to know what the child was saying, but the animated gestures and conversational patter made Zoe smile.

"My goodness, I'll bet you are just the smartest little girl ever, aren't you?" A moment of silence echoed the child's agreement. "Look, we're in the men's department already. Maybe your Daddy's here and he lost track of you. Sometimes that happens with Dads." At least she hoped that was what had happened. Where could her parents be?

* * *

Bradley stood in the men's department, looking at ties while his mind was busy with family affairs. Driving to the mall after visiting his sister Rhonda and her husband Pete, he'd experienced a mixture of love and disdain for them. He loved his sister, he really did, but he couldn't understand their lifestyle. Pete was a low paid carpenter, while Rhonda was a stay-at-home mother to multitudes of children who were not her own.

Pete and Rhonda's habit of caring for foster children was reflected in their home furnishings. Shabby and well-worn, the furniture had withstood years of children jumping, spilling, drooling, and God knew what else.

I wish they would at least let me buy them a new living room set. It's so embarrassing to see how they live, in that tiny little house, but Rhonda won't listen to me. Ever. She just laughs every time I suggest it.

Absently fingering the multi-colored ties on the rack in front of him, Bradley looked up. Across the store stood a perky young woman with a child in her arms. Startled, he froze.

I know her.

He must have seen her somewhere before, but he couldn't think where. A rush of heat raced through him as he stared at the shoulder length red hair curling around her face.

Why does she look so familiar? Am I having some kind of déjà-vu?

She was what would be described as interesting looking, dressed in a bright, bohemian style that was the exact opposite of what Bradley looked for in a woman. The hippy-dippy style was not for him.

She's beautiful.

He was confused by his reaction; Bradley was not the type of man to indulge in an instant attraction, regardless of the woman, but especially attraction toward someone with a style like that. He preferred sleek, not folksy.

Perhaps he'd seen her at this mall before or shopping somewhere else. That would explain why he thought he knew her. No reason to get all worked up over some strange woman.

Still, she intrigued him.

Her voice skipped across the store. "Look at all the Christmas decorations. Let's see, these ornaments over here are red, and this is blue… just give a holler when you see Daddy or someone, okay honey?"

Envy settled into Bradley as he listened to the woman's chatter and watched the perfect picture of mother and daughter.

* * *

Searching the aisles of each department, Zoe's apprehension mounted. The parents were nowhere to be found. "This is weird. Who leaves a kid alone in the middle of the mall?" As the girl's grip tightened around her neck, Zoe bit her lip. She hadn't meant to say that out loud.

Good thing I found her. There are lots of weird people in this world, and it's dangerous for a little girl to be alone in a mall.

A line of customers waited at the nearest cash register. Saturday was the busiest shopping day of the week, and today was no exception. Trying to catch the attention of the teenaged cashier, she stepped to the front of the line.

Shoppers responded immediately.

"Hey, no cutting!"

"Get to the end of the line, lady."

Zoe turned to the people in line, telling them, "I'm not buying anything, I just have a question."

"Yeah, well park your question in back," shot a disgruntled man waiting his turn.

Zoe's arms circled the child tighter, holding her in a protective embrace. "This is important, so I'm sure you can spare the thirty seconds it will take." Turning to the pierced cashier she asked, "I have a lost child here. Has anybody come by who's lost a child or reported anything about a missing child?"

"You'll have to go to the mall security. That's on the other side of the building, down where they've got Santa set up."

"Santa's here?" Zoe was surprised. Thanksgiving was still weeks away. Did the holidays really start this early?

"I think your thirty seconds are up," snarled the customer in line.

"There's no need to be rude." The voice was behind her.

Surprised, Zoe stared up at the man who came to her defense. Dressed in an expensive suit, he looked every bit the handsome and imposing executive type. She'd worked with men like this and tended to avoid dealing with these high powered people. Nothing good ever happened when she did business with them. His kindness impressed her. *Maybe this one is different.*

"I suppose you want to cut into the line, too," said the customer. *Nothing like a little bit of Christmas to bring out the best in people.*

"No," her new friend responded evenly. "I just don't think you have any reason to be rude to a woman and her child."

Her stomach did a flip when he looked down at her and asked, "Are you all right? Is there anything I can help you with?"

Staring into his deep blue eyes set in a classically chiseled face, Zoe had trouble finding words. That never happened. Her reaction was confusing, to say the least.

"Thank you, I'm—I mean, we're fine. We're leaving," she stammered. Heart pounding against her rib cage, she suppressed a shiver when he placed his hand on the small of her back, leading her away from the crowd and toward the door.

"It seems that people are getting a head start on their holiday rudeness," he said, frowning. Reaching the store exit that led into the mall interior, they stopped.

"Well, umm, thanks. I appreciate your concern." At that moment the child in her arms began to babble again, kicking her legs and reaching her arms out toward him.

He smiled at the little girl. "Hello, princess. Are you having a good time shopping with your mommy?"

"Oh," Zoe breathed. "I'm not her mom. I found her back in the girls' department, and I think she must be lost because nobody seems to be looking for her. I was trying to figure out where to go to help find her parents." There was a brief moment of silence as they looked at the bright little girl, happily babbling in her own language.

"I mean, somebody must be looking for her, right?" Zoe needed confirmation of this, and surely the man standing in front of her would know something. Suits like him always did.

"I would think so," he answered. "But I admit, that is a little disconcerting. Do you want me to go with you? I can help you straighten all this out."

Zoe hesitated. Although she felt a strong attraction to this very handsome stranger, she also knew that that was exactly what he was—a stranger. The child in her arms changed everything, and she couldn't wander off with the first good looking man to come along. Even one in a suit. For all she knew, he could be something terrible, like a serial killer or a stock broker.

As if sensing her hesitation, he added, "Listen, my name is Bradley Russell. I'm a vice president over at Eastboard Communications. Why don't I just walk with you to the security office?"

What's the worst that could happen? Zoe decided to go with what her instincts were telling her and to trust him. Besides, she was surrounded by people and wouldn't be alone with him. They would stay in the mall where it was safe.

"Thanks, that'd be nice. I'm Zoe Dearborn, president of Zoe's Extraordinary Beads." She said the last part with a faint smile, knowing that he wasn't the kind of man who would be familiar with her product.

They walked in silence through the mall, Bradley keeping his hand firmly on the small of Zoe's back, Zoe with the child held protectively in her arms. For some reason, this didn't bother Zoe. In fact, she liked it, the warm feeling of his hand on her. Even dressed the way he was, Mr. Bradley Russell was a handsome man. *What am I thinking? I don't pick up men at the mall. I don't pick up men, period.*

Her day had taken a decidedly unusual turn.

For a brief moment, she wondered if people thought they were a family. Trying to stop that line of thinking and break her discomfort, Zoe asked, "So, what does Eastboard Communications do?"

"Global marketing strategies. What does Zoe's Extraordinary Beads do?" He asked the question without disdain, but it still made Zoe defensive.

"I make beaded jewelry, necklaces, earrings, that kind of thing."

Bradley nodded, his face serious under the fluorescent lights. "And what does your husband do?" he asked.

Zoe bristled at the question. "What makes you think I'm married?"

"Well, you must be if that beading business is your only job. I can't imagine you could support yourself doing that. Can you?"

"For your information, yes I can, and I do very well thank you."

"I didn't mean to insult you, I just—"

"I know," Zoe interrupted, stopping in the middle of the mall. "High powered executives like you could not imagine living life the way I do. I'll bet you have a nice foreign car, and a nice condo with sleek, modern furniture. You probably take a vacation twice a year and have a girlfriend or wife who is tall and knows how to throw a proper dinner party. I'm sure you couldn't imagine living in a small apartment but absolutely loving your career or not buying designer labels but buying from a thrift shop because they have more interesting clothes."

Bradley looked like he was trying not to smile. "Do you have a cat, too?" he asked.

Zoe fumed.

"I will not even bother to answer that question. You should probably leave now." Turning on her heel, Zoe marched toward the door to the security office. It didn't matter that she did, in fact, have a cat. What mattered was the impudence with which he had asked her.

The security guard standing outside the office greeted Zoe, while Bradley stood a few yards back. *Good. Who needs him?* Without warning, the little girl in her arms let loose with a piercing wail that could be heard the entire length of the mall. Her chubby little arms reached back to Bradley.

Zoe froze. She wasn't experienced enough with children to know what this meant, and it looked like the kid was in pain. "What's wrong, honey?" she asked the little girl. She tried jiggling the child and patting her on the back, but the screams continued.

"Babababa. Ba."

"Oh, well that makes sense, then."

"Is there a problem here?" the security guard asked

"No, I mean, yes." Zoe was flustered. The child's reaction to Bradley, combined with the frustration Zoe felt toward the man and the ache in her arms made her lightheaded.

"What she means is that she would like to report a lost child." Bradley stepped forward and the child looked at him with obvious delight in her eyes.

"Just because he's handsome doesn't mean you need to fawn over him," Zoe whispered to the child. The little girl batted her eyes at Bradley, and Zoe sighed.

"Did you lose your child?" the guard asked.

"No, I found this child in a department store. I looked for her parents, but I couldn't find them, so I came here."

"Whose child is that?"

Zoe bit back a smile. The situation was far from funny but clearly the security guard was a little slow to understand what she was trying to explain.

"We don't know, we were hoping you could help us find out," Bradley answered carefully. Turning to Zoe, he told her, "Listen,

I'm sorry, I didn't mean to insult you back there. Please accept my apologies."

"I suppose." Zoe wasn't sure if she was more upset with him or with herself for feeling attracted to him. It wasn't right that she had to fight an overwhelming urge to throw herself at him, but that wasn't his fault. Besides, if the kid was any indication, Zoe wasn't the only female swooning. *Not my type, not my type…*

The guard shrugged and turned. "Yeah, sure, I'll make an announcement." Moments later his voice was heard over the mall's loudspeaker. "Attention, everyone. A lost child has been found. Will the parents of the child please report to the security office. A lost child has been found. Parents, please report to the security office."

Bradley and Zoe stood, awkwardly, waiting for someone to claim the child. Zoe's arms tightened briefly as she thought about the parents who might claim her. *Where on earth are they, and why aren't they frantically searching for her already? If this were my child, I would be out of my mind with worry by now.*

As if on cue, Bradley frowned at Zoe and said, "I can't believe her parents aren't already here or haven't at least checked with security. Someone must be looking for her."

The guard answered. "Well, no one has stopped by to report a missing child. If no one steps forward to claim this one, I'm going to have to call the police."

CHAPTER TWO

THE POLICE OFFICER TAKING THE report shuffled his feet and didn't make much eye contact. He was clearly uncomfortable.

"I know you care about what happens to the kid, but I need to get all the information before we can launch an investigation," he said.

"In the meantime, I'll take her for a walk around the mall, see if anyone is looking for her," Bradley said. This little girl did not need to hear a police officer grilling Zoe. Besides, what if her parents were in another store, still searching? Unlikely, but possible. Maybe they hadn't heard the earlier announcement.

"I'm sorry, I need you to stay here for now. Rules are rules," the officer said for the fourth time.

"Some rules inhibit progress," Zoe said, still clutching the girl.

"I'm sure her parents wouldn't want a stranger walking around with their kid," the officer said. "Now, what did you do between the time you left the store where you found her and the time you got here?"

Bradley marveled at Zoe's composure, listening as she answered the same question for the third time. Personally, he wanted to rip the note pad out of the officer's hand, but that would be counterproductive.

Still, it would feel good to at least be doing something.

"All right folks, I think I have enough information," the officer said. "Now we just have to wait for the social worker to get here and then we can all be on our way."

Zoe's face was a mask, but Bradley suspected she was trying not to cry. After all, this was not their child and they knew that. Somewhere, someone had to be missing the little girl.

Bradley cleared his throat. "Perhaps while we wait we can take the child to get some lunch. It is, after all, getting late in the day, and I'm sure she's hungry."

As if in response, the child kicked her legs and squealed, making Zoe laugh. "I think that's a great idea. Let's get her some food, and the social worker can meet us at the restaurant." She turned to the officer and pointed to where they would be eating. "Right there, you can see the restaurant from here. Just tell the social worker where he can find us." Without waiting for a response, she turned and began to walk away.

"Ma'am?" the police officer called after her. "Ma'am, I'm not sure this is such a good idea. Why don't we all wait here for the social worker?"

Zoe stared at him with a steely glint in her eyes. "Officer, I understand that you have a job to do, but this child needs food. The restaurant is only a few steps away from us. Surely you are not going to let her be neglected, are you?"

Bradley suppressed a smile as he watched the officer stammer. "Of course not, you go right ahead. I'll make sure he knows where you are."

Following Zoe, Bradley couldn't help but realize that his admiration for the woman had grown substantially. Not only was he attracted to her physically, but he loved her natural maternal instinct. She didn't hand the kid over to someone else to take care of, a trait he knew he might find in the women he usually associated with.

Once seated in the restaurant, he asked, "Do you have children of your own? You seem like such a natural mom."

Blushing, Zoe looked down at the table. "No. I've always wanted a family, but it just never happened."

"Don't you have a boyfriend?"

"Not right now. Besides, at this point it's probably too late."

Bradley was puzzled. "Too late for a boyfriend?"

"No, too late for a family. I'm going to be thirty nine years old in December."

"That's not too old. I'm the same age, and I'm still planning on having a family."

"Oh. Do you have a girlfriend, then?"

Bradley hesitated. He knew he needed to tell her the truth, but he didn't want to. His better instincts won. "Yes. Stephanie and I have been dating for quite some time now. Her father works at my company."

"Hmm. I'll bet she'll make a good corporate wife then, right?"

Bradley was unreasonably annoyed. His relationship with Stephanie was none of her business. "Stephanie has a career of her own. She's not the type to sit at home and become a corporate executive's wife." Bradley hoped his tone was enough to stop the questions, but apparently not.

"I see. And what does, um, Sofie do for a living?"

"Stephanie. She's a media relations consultant."

"Right. Stephanie." The food arrived, and Zoe was busy cutting the child's chicken into small pieces. "Here sweetheart, do you know how to use a spoon? I'll help you with the applesauce."

Bradley was silent, watching Zoe feed the little girl. "What do you think her name is?"

"Abigail."

"Wow, that was quick. What made you think of that?"

Zoe shrugged. "I don't know, it just seems like I've been thinking of her as Abby. You know, short for Abigail. She looks like that would be her name."

Bradley stared at the child. Zoe was right; she did look like an Abby. "Okay, then let's call her Abby."

Zoe's face was wistful. "At least we can call her that for as long as she's with us. What do you think will happen?"

Bradley hesitated. A piece of an idea had come to him while they were talking to the police, but he didn't want to say anything. Instead, he was waiting for the social worker.

"I don't want to say too much to get your hopes up, but I may have an idea."

"Do you think they'll let her come home with me?" Bradley knew that Zoe was trying hard not to cry, especially in front of Abby. She wouldn't let the little girl see her dismay.

Bradley hated to tell her, but he had to be honest. He hoped Zoe would think this was an attractive quality, but it was probably too soon for him to think about that. He had no right, yet, to pursue a relationship. "No, I doubt it. That's not usually how social services operates."

"Indeed it's not. Indeed." Bradley and Zoe looked up from their meal to find an older, round, and slightly disheveled man standing before them.

Bradley blinked. He'd never seen a man quite so… gray. Clothes and hair Bradley could understand, but this guy's skin had a washed-out tone, as if he never went outside or lived under fluorescent lights only.

"Forgive the interruption, but I assume you two are um, let me see…" Pulling a pair of half spectacles down from a graying head of hair, he removed a piece of paper from his bulging briefcase and read, "Zoe Dearborn and Bradley Russell?" At their affirmative nods, he smiled and extended a hand to Zoe and Bradley in turn.

Bradley shook his hand, feeling comfortable with the social worker despite his unfortunate coloring.

"Wonderful, lovely to meet you both, truly wonderful," he boomed. "I'm Percy, the case worker assigned to you. Why don't we sit and talk for a moment."

Percy sat next to Bradley in the booth, smiling at Abby. "Well, hello there. What are we eating today?"

Abby's face broke into a large smile and she began chattering away to the man, waving her forkful of chicken as she spoke. Percy listened for a moment, nodding. "I see," he told her. Turning to Zoe and Bradley, he said, "Our young friend here says you have been taking very good care of her. Let's talk about what's going to happen next."

Bradley cleared his throat before speaking. "Actually, Percy, I kind of have an idea."

CHAPTER THREE

THE SUN HAD SET LONG before Bradley arrived home. His condominium was situated on the water, providing spectacular views of Virginia Beach. Pulling into his garage, it hit him. He didn't look out his windows anymore. He never saw the spectacular sunrises over the water that the realtor had promised he'd love or the sweep of white sand just beyond his doorstep. His mornings were focused on getting to work on time, so he no longer heard the cry of the gulls outside or smelled the salt in the air. His days were always busy, leaving no time for that kind of thing.

It's late and it's dark and I paid a huge amount of money for a place I barely live in. It's all for show. Zoe was right about me.

Exhausted, he climbed the steps into his living space, took off his coat and threw it over a dining room chair. Loosening his tie, he sank into the couch, throwing his head back onto the cushions and shutting his eyes.

"Don't close your eyes just yet, darling. We have reservations tonight, remember? Where on earth have you been, anyway?"

Keeping his eyes closed, Bradley answered. "Stephanie, can't we just eat in tonight? Maybe have a home cooked meal for a change?"

He felt her pout before he saw it. Standing at the granite topped island that separated the kitchen from the living space, his girlfriend impatiently tapped her manicured nails.

"Bradley, what are you talking about? We're supposed to go to the opening of the new Cambodian restaurant downtown tonight. It's important for us to go, we need to be seen. Really, a home cooked meal? Like a casserole made with cream of mushroom soup? What's gotten into you?"

Sighing, he opened his eyes and got up from the couch. Walking to her, he planted a kiss on her cheek. "You're right. I'm just tired. It's been a long and really weird day."

Stephanie's cat-like green eyes narrowed at him. Standing at five feet nine inches in her stiletto heels, she wore an obviously expensive little black dress for the evening. "You must have visited your sister."

Irritation flashed through Bradley. "Yes, that was part of it. She's doing well, by the way, and sends her regards."

"I'm sure. How are all the little monsters?"

Normally Bradley would find this amusing, but tonight was different. For the first time in a long time, he was offended on behalf of his sister. "They're okay, you know, they're just kids. Rhonda and Pete do the best they can with them."

Stephanie shuddered. "I cannot imagine having so many children climbing all over my house. Anyway, do hurry dear, we don't want to be late."

Bradley stopped, staring at his girlfriend. She hadn't changed; she was still the same woman she had always been. Beautiful, sophisticated and a bit of a snob, Stephanie was what he always thought he wanted in a woman. *Maybe I've changed. Maybe this whole crazy day has somehow changed who I am. For better or worse, now's the time to get this out in the open.*

"Stephanie, I know we've never talked about this before, but I need to ask you something."

"Now?"

"Yes, now."

"Is this going to be a marriage proposal?" Stephanie's eyes glittered.

"No, but it's something we need to discuss if we're thinking about marriage. Would you ever be interested in starting a family, having children?"

Stephanie took a long, slow breath before answering. "Bradley, you know that my career is the most important part of my life right now." Seeing the look on his face, she hurried to add, "Outside of you, of course."

"Of course," he muttered.

"I have to say that I don't see myself staying home, playing mommy, stewing tomatoes every day and wiping up snot and God knows what else. I thought you understood that—my career comes first. And now that it looks like I'll be up for another promotion, well, even if I wanted children, I don't think I'd have the time."

"I see." And he did. Bradley understood exactly what Stephanie was saying: that she had not in fact changed at all. He also realized something important about himself.

"Well, Steph, I want a family. I want kids, and I would love to have a wife who stayed home to care for them. I won't settle for less."

Stephanie stared at him coolly. "Then, Bradley, I would say that you and I have a problem. A serious problem."

* * *

"So it's over, just like that?" Rhonda's excited voice bounced through the phone lines.

"Thanks for the show of sympathy, sis," Bradley said. "Anyway, I'm sorry to be calling so late, I hope I didn't wake you." It was after eleven, but he'd taken a chance his sister was still awake. "I had to let you know everything that happened today so you'd be ready for tomorrow."

"Oh, don't worry, everything is all set. Abby is here right now. She's asleep."

"Already?" Bradley was surprised. He'd hoped his sister could take Abby, but he knew that sometimes regulations and legal restrictions prevailed.

"Yeah, I guess Percy was pretty impressed when he checked our records because he called us right away. I almost couldn't believe the story he told me. Is it true you were at the mall with a woman and you two just found this little thing? All by herself?"

"Well, that's sort of how it happened. Actually, Zoe found Abby, I just found Zoe."

"Zoe?"

"Yes, and she's a really great person. In fact, I think you're going to like her when you meet her."

Bradley knew his sister would embrace Zoe in a way she'd never been able to do with Stephanie. For one thing, Zoe was much warmer, nicer, prettier…

"I get to meet her? Is this the real reason why you broke up with Stephanie?" Rhonda's voice intruded.

The image of Zoe was already in Bradley's head, her red hair and creamy skin, her soft curves and delicious scent. After only the short amount of time he'd spent with her, he couldn't stop thinking about the woman. He'd never known this kind of attraction and wasn't sure what to do with it.

"Bradley?" his sister interrupted his thoughts.

"No, Stephanie and I had a little talk, and I guess I figured out that we're not as compatible as I thought we were."

"Well, hallelujah to that is what I say." Rhonda's voice was firm. "She was no good for you. So, if this Zoe has nothing to do with your break up, why am I going to meet her?"

"She got really attached to Abby today, and I think she feels responsible for what happens to the little girl. And I wanted to warn you, she's applying to become a foster parent, too. She wants Abby to live with her."

"Did she tell you that she wanted Abby to live with her?" Rhonda asked.

"She didn't exactly put it into words, but I saw the look on her face when Percy took Abby away. I think it kind of tore her up inside. She just turned to me and started crying."

"Poor kid." Rhonda's voice was sympathetic. "I know how it is, you get attached to the little ones and then something happens. I hope it works out, for her sake."

Bradley was startled to realize what a generous woman Rhonda was. Most people would be selfishly worried about their own claim on the child, but with a rare flash of insight he realized his sister wasn't like that. She'd want only what was best for Abby.

How could anyone not want that child to have the best of everything? She was sweet and innocent and sure as hell didn't deserve being abandoned in a shopping mall.

His sister's voice broke into his thoughts. "Of course Zoe can come over anytime. I'd love to meet her. Does she know where we live?"

Bradley hesitated. "Actually, she asked me to pick her up tomorrow and take her to your house. I hope that's okay with you."

Rhonda laughed. "Good, she's a mama bear who knows what she wants. Well, you can come on over after breakfast. We'll be here."

Bradley was touched and maybe even a little embarrassed.

"Thanks, Rhonda. I'll see you tomorrow." Perhaps he'd been wrong about his sister all these years.

CHAPTER FOUR

ZOE'S NEIGHBORHOOD IN NORFOLK WAS sometimes referred to as transitional. Not quite the outskirts of town where crime and poverty reigned, but close enough to the edges of that to maintain that simultaneous juxtaposition of shabby yet vibrant. Lawns weren't always mowed, but neighborhood grocers offered a wider variety of ethnic foods not carried by the local chains. House colors ranged from white to shocking blue, as there was no historical zoning in effect here to keep everything muted. Zoe's house—which she had decided to purchase because of the arched doorways and floor to ceiling windows allowing so much light in—was divided into three apartments, and the rent from the two tenants mostly paid her mortgage. Decorated in a style that was pure Zoe, it was her sanctuary.

Curled on her couch, Zoe stared at the night sky outside her window. She knew she had work to do, but couldn't get motivated. Despite what Bradley had hinted at earlier, Zoe's

Extraordinary Beads did a tremendous business. Her three full-time and two part-time employees kept pace with the steady flow of orders. The success of the business was due largely to her outrageous designs; Zoe Dearborn was known for successfully pairing unlikely colors and using non-traditional design patterns in her work. Her artistic talent was evident in her creations, and her common sense helped build a successful business.

Tonight, though, her mind was preoccupied with thoughts of two people: Abby and Bradley. It was obvious to her why she was consumed with thoughts of the little girl—after all, she was a child alone in the world. How had that happened? How does a child end up alone in a mall, with no one to claim her? Was there an irresponsible babysitter or nanny involved? Zoe shuddered at the thought of anyone else finding the girl. *There's lots of weird people out there, thank God I found her when I did.*

Her other thoughts were more confusing. The feelings Bradley evoked were unexpected, to say the least. To her surprise, she'd had fun spending time with him. Despite the obvious physical attraction, she loved that Bradley expressed an interest in her thoughts and opinions during lunch. They had talked late into the afternoon, even after Percy had taken Abby to her foster home.

"I can't believe he has a sister who takes care of foster children," Zoe told her tortoise-shell cat who lay curled against her. "Maybe I shouldn't have been so dismissive of him and his whole corporate lifestyle."

She closed her eyes and rubbed them. Whatever attraction she felt for the man didn't matter. He had a girlfriend, so that was the end of that. Zoe was not a woman who went after other people's men, and she wasn't interested in being with someone who cheated.

Absently petting her cat, the burn of unshed tears stung her eyes. "It's so weird, I almost felt like we were a real family. I miss

Abby, but I miss Bradley, too. How could I have feelings for him so quickly?"

At least the cat listens to me. Reaching for a bag of chips, Zoe said, "I have a feeling this is going to be a very long night."

* * *

Zoe was unable to sleep, and finally gave up and got out of bed as the first light of dawn crept into her room. Taking her time, she had a leisurely breakfast and read the morning newspaper from cover to cover, including the classifieds. Her cat watched silently from his window perch, ears periodically twitching at something Zoe would read aloud.

"There's nothing in here, nothing at all. I don't know why I thought there would be," she announced to the feline as she refolded the paper. "I guess I had an image of a front page article, something that said, 'Little Girl Missing, Mother Frantic'. They must not have found her family yet."

Again, Zoe wondered about that. Someone had to be out there who cared about the girl. If Zoe had ever wandered off in a store when she was a kid her mother would've torn the place apart looking for her.

Telling herself there was no real reason for it, Zoe took extra care as she got ready for the day. She picked a flattering outfit to wear, a long, slim green skirt topped with a soft, cream sweater that hugged her curves. She was careful to use the right products on her hair and applied just the right amount of makeup.

"Not that it matters," she reminded herself. "He's got a girlfriend."

At exactly eleven that morning, her doorbell rang. Looking out the peephole, she saw a smiling Bradley waving at her. Opening the door, she laughed. "How did you know I was looking through the peep hole?"

"It's what I expected you to do," he answered, entering her

apartment. He seemed at ease, his presence filling the space. It was hard for her to breathe with him taking up all the air around her. "Are you ready to go?"

Zoe nervously took in Bradley's casual look, jeans and a sweater with a brown leather jacket. He smelled good, too, a combination of some type of soap and cologne.

"I'm ready when you are," she said, and immediately blushed, hating that her feelings were probably so obvious.

"I'm ready right now," Bradley whispered, taking a step toward her. Without warning, he leaned over and allowed his lips to meet hers. His kiss was gentle at first, softly grazing her lips. There was no mistaking the intent.

Zoe took a step back, reeling. "Okay, wow. What was that all about? Don't you have a girlfriend, Sandy or something?"

Bradley's face was serious as he looked into her eyes. "No. Her name was Stephanie, but we split up."

"Really? And exactly when did that happen?" Zoe wasn't born yesterday, and she wasn't about to let herself get duped into a relationship with a cheater.

"It happened last night when I got home. We had a little conversation about what we wanted out of life and decided it was time to go our separate ways. I think it was a long time coming, I just hadn't realized it. Now, are you ready to go see Abby?"

Zoe stared at him for a moment, then consciously closed her mouth. She believed him about his break up, but wasn't certain what that meant for her. "Let's go," she said decisively. There would be plenty of time later to think about Bradley and the fact that he was now single.

The drive to Rhonda's house didn't take long. Zoe adjusted her skirt as they stood at the front door. Bradley knocked, opened the door and entered. Rhonda was warm and welcoming, and they were barely inside the house when Abby ran to sit with Zoe, babbling non-stop in her own language.

"How did she sleep last night? Did she eat a good breakfast?" Zoe's anxiety about the girl's well-being was soon dispelled by Rhonda.

"She slept very well, and she ate a pretty big breakfast. She has a room all to herself, would you like to see it?"

Walking through the small house, Zoe couldn't help but admire this couple and all that they did. It was obvious they didn't have a lot of money, but it seemed to Zoe that the feeling of warmth and comfort in their home more than made up for that fact.

"I love your sister and her husband, it's great here," she whispered to Bradley a few minutes later.

With a wry smile, he answered, "I'm so glad you think so. It's taken me a while, but I have to agree with you."

"So what are you kids going to do today?" Rhonda called from the other room.

"Do?" Bradley wasn't sure what she meant.

"Well, yes, silly. You three don't want to sit around here all day. Why don't you go to the park or something?" Rhonda walked back into the room with a bowl of chips. "There's no reason to hang out with us, you'll have more fun if you take Abby out for a while. What do you think, Pete?"

Her husband, Pete, answered with a smile toward his wife. "I think whatever you think, sweetheart."

"Take your coats, it's chilly outside. Just be sure to come back by four, that's when Percy's stopping by for a visit."

Bemused, Zoe and Bradley got Abby into her coat and walked outside toward the car. Barely a moment passed before Rhonda opened the front door and called after them, "Don't forget to take the car seat out of my car for her."

* * *

Closing the door with a satisfied smile, Rhonda looked at her husband sitting in his chair across the room. "I don't know how it happened, but I feel like I just got my brother back. I think this is going to be perfect, don't you?"

Pete shook his head at her. "Don't get your little matchmaking hopes up yet. You never know. He could still change his mind and go back to life with Suzy."

"Stephanie."

"Whatever her name was. Your brother's a great guy, don't get me wrong, but he lives differently than us."

Rhonda wasn't listening. "It's obvious that they have feelings for each other, you can just tell when they're in the same room together. I mean, geez Louise, the air around them sizzles. Reminds me of one of them romance books. Maybe we can have a June wedding."

Pete didn't answer. He knew enough to know that he wasn't going to change his wife's mind. Besides, a June wedding was just fine with him.

* * *

Zoe couldn't remember the last time she had so much fun. The three of them walked through the park, stopping to play at the playground. Bradley and Zoe climbed the equipment with Abby, and all three of them went down the slide. Later, they found a small snack shack that sold big, warm pretzels and laughed as they ordered first one, then another, and finally a third.

Walking around, Abby toddled in front of them, babbling and pointing at birds, people and trees. Bradley reached for Zoe, holding her hand firmly.

"I like this," he told her.

"Me too." Zoe felt no apprehension about this man but was pierced by a wave of longing so intense it took her breath away. Was it this man in particular she wanted, or was it the safety of a family? Part of her felt the need for caution, the need to protect herself from possible hurt. The other part of her wanted to run away with Bradley.

"Maybe after we bring Abby home and talk to Percy we could get some dinner." Bradley's voice sounded husky.

Zoe didn't hesitate. "That would be great. Your place or mine?" Her boldness surprised her, but then everything about this situation surprised her. She'd never known a man like Bradley who had such a strong effect on her. She was comfortable with him, he made her laugh, and she wanted him in a physical way that left her aching. Yep, she had it bad.

Leaning in to kiss her, Bradley said, "I think that the way I feel right now even the car would be just fine."

"We'll go to your place, this way I'll get to see all that fancy chrome and granite."

"How do you know that's what my place looks like?"

Zoe smiled. "I already know lots about you, Bradley."

"Good. Just as long as you understand that I'm planning on us getting to know each other even better. Much better."

* * *

Bradley, Zoe, and Abby got back to the house a little before four o'clock. Sitting in the living room, they laughed together as they told Rhonda about their day. At times, Rhonda had to ask what they were talking about, claiming she couldn't understand them because they were both talking at the same time, or one was laughing while the other spoke. Mixed in with this was Abby's excited chatter as she shared her own perspective on the afternoon.

A knock on the door stopped all conversation. Zoe's stomach tightened as Rhonda let Percy in. *Has he found them? Has he found Abby's parents?* Zoe's mind whirled with the ramifications of what that would mean for her. *If he did, I might never see Abby again.* Zoe knew the child belonged with her parents, but her heart said otherwise. It was going to be hard enough leaving her overnight at Rhonda's house, she couldn't imagine never seeing

Abby again.

Despite her misgivings, Percy's presence calmed her. She noted his unfortunate gray pallor, wondering why he would choose clothes that mirrored that particular shade of dismal. Despite all the gray, he exuded a warmth that put Zoe at ease.

Percy walked straight to Abby, beaming. "Hello again, little one. How was your day today?"

Without hesitation, Abby looked up at Percy and launched into her own version of the day's events. It sounded like babble to everyone in the room, but Percy listened carefully and nodded.

"The playground, eh? And you had a pretzel? Three pretzels?"

Zoe leaned in to Bradley. "How can he do that? How does he understand her?"

"I don't know," he whispered. "Some people are just good with kids, I guess."

Percy laughed at something Abby said before gesturing to the adults. "Why don't we go into the kitchen?" he suggested. "She wants to watch her television show out here."

As they all filed into the kitchen, Zoe looked back. Indeed, Abby was engrossed in an episode of *Daniel Tiger*, content to stay in the living room.

Sitting around the large picnic table where meals were served in the kitchen, everyone stared expectantly at Percy. He cleared his throat before speaking. "First of all, you should know that every effort is being made to locate the parents. Unfortunately, it's not that easy. We have nothing to go on right now, so we're at a loss. The police want to release some of this information to the press to see if anyone comes forward."

Zoe tried to swallow past the lump in her throat.

"And what happens when you do find her parents?" Bradley's voice was angry. "Do they get to just take her back? That doesn't seem like such a good option for Abby. Who deserts their kid in a mall, anyway?"

Percy nodded. "I know, I know, it's not a good situation. If the parents can be located then of course we would step in to assess the situation. But right now we're also looking at another possibility."

"I don't like the sound of this," Rhonda said.

"You're going to like it less when you hear this," Percy told them. "Last night police found evidence outside the mall that there may have been a crime committed." He hesitated, shifting with discomfort in his chair. "There was a large amount of blood found by a dumpster out back."

"Did they find a body?" Pete asked.

Percy shook his head. "No, not yet, but according to police whoever lost that amount of blood would be unlikely to survive. Now, remember, there may or may not be a connection between that and Abby, but we won't know for sure until we find out who got hurt back there. But it's possible that this little girl witnessed a crime that involved her parent or parents."

Zoe wrapped her arms around herself to stop from shivering. This was far from good news. "Is she in any danger?"

"We don't think so," Percy answered. "Nobody knows that she's here, and we think this is the safest place for her."

"We're going to be here as much as possible, so we'll be able to keep an eye on her." Bradley sounded determined. "Nobody is going to get to her, not while I have anything to say about it."

Despite the situation, Rhonda grinned at her brother. "I've never seen you take such an interest in kids before."

Bradley's eyes were grim. "This is different. Abby is family. I don't know how to explain it, but she is."

Zoe nodded. "That's right. Rhonda, if you don't mind, maybe we can set up a schedule so that we can spend more time with Abby. I don't want to get in your way, but I'd like to be here when I can."

Percy nodded. "That would be fine with me. Do you mean both

of you, or just one of you?"

"Both of us," Bradley and Zoe answered.

Percy smiled brightly at the group. "This is perfect, just perfect. Don't worry, everything is going to turn out exactly the way it's supposed to."

CHAPTER FIVE

"YOU'VE HAD SOME CRAZY IDEAS before, but this one is beyond crazy. I think you need to take a step back and re-think this whole thing. I mean, this is your life you're talking about, right? And not just your life, but a child's life, too." Zoe was on her couch, listening as her friend Maggie's well-meaning voice came through the phone.

Staring at the lights on her Christmas tree, she said, "Mags, I get that you're worried, I really do. If it were you, I'd be worried too. I just don't see any other way to do this."

Her cat jumped up to the window, eyeing the Christmas tree ornaments. There were so many holiday decorations for him to destroy, it was simply a question of what he was going to wreak havoc on next. Zoe picked up her *Seasons Greetings* throw pillow and launched it at the cat while she listened to Maggie. Not that it did any good to throw a pillow at a cat, but she had to try.

"Let's go over this again. You and Bradley have gotten to know each other really well in the past few weeks, right?"

"Right." Although Maggie couldn't see it, Zoe blushed at the comment. The first night they had sex was burned into her memory as one of the most erotic moments of her lifetime. It didn't end there, either. It seemed they were always thinking up new ways to tantalize each other, ways that resulted in losing many nights of sleep.

"And you both care about this little girl who has no parents, right? Are the police positive there are no other relatives?"

Zoe remembered the night Percy delivered the news. Sitting at Rhonda's kitchen table, he sadly shook his head and told them Abby's mother had been murdered, her body found in the trunk of a car. They had a lead on the murderers and were working the case, but now Abby was without a mother.

"There was no father listed on the birth certificate, and the mother had no family to speak of. Percy put an ad in the paper looking for relatives, but no one has come forward. Percy moved pretty quickly to terminate parental rights, so even if there is a father out there he has no claim on her. Abby is legally available for adoption."

"Why don't you adopt her?" Maggie demanded.

Zoe hesitated. She knew that explaining this part would be difficult, but she had to try. "Percy told us that a judge was more likely to award custody to a married couple rather than a single person. He said that being married really helped in cases like this."

"He didn't mean you had to run out and get married right now!" Maggie exploded. "You haven't even known Bradley that long, not long enough for a lifetime commitment, that's for sure."

Zoe knew her friend meant well. "Maggie, listen. This is different. I'm almost forty years old, I've dated a few men in my life. But this time I know, I really know, that Bradley is the man I've been waiting for. There is no question in my mind that I want to spend the rest of my life with him, so this makes perfect sense to me."

"Does Bradley know about this?"

Zoe hesitated. "No, not yet. I think he has the same feelings for me since he's told me he loves me, but I haven't discussed this with him yet."

"So your plan is to go over there tonight and ask him to marry you so you two can adopt Abby?"

Zoe grinned."Yep, that's the plan. Wish me luck."

Maggie sighed. "I have to say I envy you. I've never heard you talk about someone like this before, and I have no doubt you love him. I don't think you'll need luck, I think you already had luck when you found each other at the mall."

"Thanks, Maggie, that means a lot to me. I'll call you tomorrow and let you know what happens."

"Forget that. You better call me tonight, I don't care what time it is."

Zoe laughed. "Okay, it's a deal. Just don't yell at me when I wake you up."

* * *

Nothing ever goes according to plan. This was usually the case, but Zoe never had things go so wrong so fast. When she got to the house her excited anticipation quickly dropped to full blown dread.

As she climbed the front steps to Rhonda's house, Bradley threw the door open. "Do you have Abby?"

"What? No, isn't she here?" Bradley's words weren't making sense to Zoe.

"No, we can't find her and we've searched everywhere." Bradley stood in the doorway, white faced and trembling. "She was outside on the swings one minute, gone the next. I only came inside for one second, to get her a juice box, and…"

"Have you called the police?" Zoe asked.

Bradley nodded. "They're on their way."

Zoe couldn't take her eyes off Bradley. This couldn't be happening, it just couldn't. Where could her baby be?

"Let's check the neighborhood."

"I've already done that, did you think I wouldn't look for her?" Bradley's voice had an edge of hysteria.

Zoe took a deep breath. "I know you would've done that. Let's do it again. Sometimes kids hide."

Bradley ran a hand through his hair, looking like he'd aged ten years in a day.

"Okay, we'll split up."

Zoe heard the sirens. Thank God, help would be here soon.

"Let them know we're out looking," Zoe said to Rhonda, who was standing behind Bradley. She took off at a sprint across the yard, yelling for Abby.

Zoe stopped after a few minutes, trying to ignore the panic that was building. If she were Abby, where would she go and why would she hide? Zoe could hear Bradley's voice in the distance. He'd gone the opposite way, trying to cover as much ground as possible. She could see the uniformed patrolmen knocking on neighbor's doors. Hopefully someone knew something.

Crossing through a yard to get to a parallel street, Zoe hesitated. It was probably a waste of time to keep searching the neighborhood. Bradley and the police would take care of this area. Turning and running back to her car, Zoe clutched her keys and prayed. *Let me find her.*

* * *

The mall was only a few miles from Rhonda's house. It was hard to believe only a few weeks ago she hadn't known Abby or Bradley. Now, she didn't want to live without either of them. Stepping out of the car, she scanned the parking lot and tried to remember what Percy had said. *Abby's mother was murdered and left in the trunk of a car. Had she been murdered inside the mall, or outside, and why was she killed?*

Zoe shivered, wondering if whoever did this to Abby's mother was looking for Abby. Could the little girl have seen something?

Slamming her car door, she began to half-jog past the rows of cars. Zoe's plan was to check the entire parking area before going into the mall. Increasing her speed, she ignored the knot of pain settling in her stomach. Something was very wrong, and Zoe could almost hear the ticking of a clock, telling her she was running out of time.

It took ten achingly long minutes before she spotted the dark sedan parked at the edge of the lot. In that moment, Zoe knew. "Abby," she whispered, and began to run.

CHAPTER SIX

BRADLEY DIDN'T KNOW WHAT THE hell Zoe was doing, but he trusted her. Seeing her run to her car and tear out of the driveway, he grabbed Officer Randall, the police officer standing next to him.

"She knows something, let's go."

When there's a missing child, nobody hesitates. With Bradley in the front seat of the patrol car, the officer radioed for backup.

"She's going to the mall," Bradley muttered.

"Why would she do that?" Officer Randall asked.

"It's where we found her. The little girl."

"Is this the kid whose mother got killed here?"

Bradley nodded grimly. "Yeah."

"Damn. I hope your girlfriend's wrong about this."

Bradley stared out the window, trying to control his emotions. "Me too."

As the car circled the parking lot, the two men strained to look through the rows of parked vehicles.

Zoe, where are you? Where's Abby?

"There, she's right there…," Bradley shouted, pointing to the dark car that Zoe was running toward.

Jumping out before Officer Randall could come to a complete stop, Bradley broke into a run.

A moment later, he heard it. Gunshots.

* * *

Bradley wondered if he was having a reaction to recent events. Almost losing Abby and Zoe had made him realize what was truly important. When the gun had fired, he'd gone a little crazy. Events in his mind were still foggy, but the one thing he clearly remembered was tackling the thug with the gun.

Bradley paced up and down Rhonda's kitchen. "What if I'm wrong? What if this is a really bad idea?"

Rhonda stood and put a hand on his shoulder. "For heaven's sake, sit down already, you're wearing a hole in the floor. Why would this be such a bad idea?"

Bradley hesitated. "Maybe I'm having some sort of post-traumatic stress reaction. Everything seems so perfect, almost too perfect."

Rhonda laughed. "Don't worry, that will go away with time."

"It will?"

"Sure it will. There's going to come a point where you two annoy each other, or she yells at you for leaving your socks on the floor, or you wonder why she didn't have time to do laundry when she was home all day. The perfect part doesn't last forever, but the other part does."

"What other part?"

"The friend part. Knowing that the person you married is your best friend and you can tell them anything. Feeling like you have someone in your life you can count on, someone who will listen to you, that's the other part. Pete and I might fight about dishes left in the sink, but at the end of the day he's the person I tell my secrets to."

Bradley stared at his sister for a moment. "You know, I never really gave you guys enough credit, and I'm sorry for that. All I ever saw was what your house looked like, or I couldn't understand why you wouldn't let me buy you things. You don't need things, do you? I'm so sorry for all those times I acted like an ass."

Rhonda hugged her brother. "Don't worry about it, you're family and I love you anyway. But now that you've seen the light, maybe I'll let you buy me a new living room set."

The sound of the doorbell stopped him from answering her. From the kitchen, he could hear Pete letting Zoe in the house. At the sound of Zoe's voice, Abby ran into the kitchen, hands waving in the air to be picked up and a smile on her face.

"Well, look who's up from her nap," Rhonda exclaimed. "Let me just get you cleaned up a little—"

"No," Bradley interrupted. "I can't stand it much longer, I can't wait. I would really like her to be here for this."

"Be here for what?" Zoe asked, walking into the kitchen.

Rhonda looked at Zoe, worried. "How are you feeling?"

"Fine, it was nothing. The bullet barely scratched my skin." Zoe shuddered. "I just can't bear to think about—"

"Don't," Bradley interrupted. "The worst is over. They're gone."

"What if—"

"No 'what ifs'." Bradley was adamant. "The stolen drugs were recovered, nobody has any reason to look for us or Abby anymore."

"I still don't understand why they thought they had to take Abby," Rhonda said, shaking her head. "For goodness sake, she's not even two years old. She still can't speak in complete sentences yet."

"Another smart criminal," Zoe said drily. "The world's full of them."

Bradley hastened to reassure everyone. "The police issued a very public statement about the whole thing, and they have no reason to bother us anymore. Plus, everyone connected to this thing is in jail. We're safe."

Zoe shuddered. "For now. Hey, what's Abby supposed to be here for?"

Bradley cleared his throat. "Zoe, you know that you and Abby mean the world to me."

"Mama." Abby squirmed, eyes big, and reached out to Zoe.

"Oh, sweetheart." Zoe's eyes filled with tears as she scooped the child into her arms.

"Dada." This time Abby was looking straight at Bradley.

Laughing, he nodded. "That's right, Abby, that's what I'm trying to do." Getting down on one knee, he looked up at Zoe.

"Zoe Dearborn, will you marry me?"

There was a silence in the kitchen as Zoe stood there, trying to catch her breath. Finally, unable to stand it any longer, she answered.

"Yes."

"Yes," Abby echoed, looking at Zoe.

"And of course we're going to apply to adopt you, sweetheart," Bradley told the little girl, standing and circling his arms around both his girls.

"I don't think that will be a problem at all." Percy's voice boomed through the kitchen.

"Percy, when did you get here?" Rhonda asked.

"Oh, I've been watching for a while now," the social worker answered. "And I couldn't think of a better ending than this one. Will you have a Christmas wedding?"

Zoe smiled. "I think that would be perfect. A simple Christmas wedding."

Bradley frowned at Zoe. "There's just… I'm sorry, things have been so crazy I didn't get you a ring, and I wasn't sure what you

wanted…"
"Bradley, I've gotten exactly what I wanted, don't worry."
"And what is that, young lady?" Percy asked.
"I've gotten a family for Christmas," Zoe answered.

CHAPTER SEVEN

THE STRAINS OF A SOFT melody could be heard as the last of the holiday workers filed into the clearing. The faint light of dawn had just started to wake into the space, revealing row after row of the gray people. Some could barely be seen as their image shimmered in the soft light. There was an excitement in the air at the possibilities in this post-Christmas meeting.

"Okay, everybody, okay, let's get started," Gabe called. "First of all, I want to say to all of you, excellent work this year, excellent. We had an extremely successful program again, and that's because of your hard work. From the list I have, it looks like I'll be taking some of you back with me this time. Now, let's talk about what happened."

"I have to say, I always enjoy the chance we're given to redeem ourselves. I know I wasted a lifetime through my indifference, but I'm starting to feel like I might be making up for that," Percy said. "This assignment was especially touching, too."

Gabe nodded. "Yes, earth is a marvelous place. Now tell me, you had the orphaned girl and the couple, right?"

"Yes. So sad that the mother had to leave her daughter, but obviously it was for the best. The mother died in a drug deal gone bad, and that is no way to raise a child."

"She's with us, now, and she's recovering nicely," Gabe's assistant, Cleo, piped in from the other side of the room. "Lovely woman, really. I think she just lost her way."

Most of the gray figures in the room nodded, being all too familiar with the ways that the humans got lost. After all, they themselves had once been human. Lifetimes lived without caring, days slipping by without purpose, it all added up to an afterlife of in-between. These were the ones who hovered, the beings who were not yet allowed to cross over after death. Their purpose now was to make up for all that. Some, like Percy, were diligent in making amends. Although he could've moved on, Percy chose to remain earthbound. The joy in helping others was too much for him to resist, and he found a satisfaction when working these assignments that he'd never found during his human life.

Others wandered, still lost.

"It's a good thing those folks didn't know much about the law, though," Percy added. "There were a few times I had to sort of stretch things to make everything work out the way it was supposed to."

"You didn't break the rules, did you?" Gabe asked, frowning.

"No, of course not, I just spent some time convincing judges and agencies to do things a certain way, that's all. No rules were broken."

"Good."

Percy sighed. "I was especially glad they got this child as it seems Zoe won't be having any others."

"What makes you say that?" Gabe demanded.

"She said she was too old to bear children."

Gabe let loose with a laugh. "Humans are so funny. They have these ideas of what their lives are going to be like, and they never seem to get it right."

"You mean that's not true?" Percy asked, hopeful. Bradley and Zoe were so good with the child, it would be a shame if they didn't have more.

"No, it's not true," Gabe answered. "In fact, let me see…" Consulting a clipboard in his hand, he looked up at Percy. "We've got a birth scheduled to Zoe in August of their time. In fact, oh my… It looks like you're going to have quite an interesting assignment with those two in a few years, Percy."

Percy was confused. "A few years? What could possibly be happening by then?"

"Twins."

A Life for Christmas

CHAPTER ONE

THE LAST THING HE REMEMBERED was getting killed. There had to be something that happened after that, like a doctor saving him or angels and harps. Or fire and brimstone. Something.

Everything's dark, he thought. Not exactly what he'd expected from death. Then he opened his eyes to the storm clouds that threatened the sky above him.

I don't remember reading about this part. Cade didn't feel dead, but there was nothing in his memory to suggest otherwise. A gunshot to the heart would, at the very least, land him in the hospital.

A biting wind stirred his longish hair, and although the ground was cold beneath him it didn't bother him. That was unusual, as he normally hated winter weather of any sort. Confused, he sat up. *This is starting to look familiar.*

"Numerous old ships are buried in that river," a voice behind him said. Cade scrambled to his feet, his hand automatically reaching for his gun that was not there. An older man sat on a park bench, looking out over the water. "When the Americans chased the English out of here, many of the vessels sank."

"Who are you?" Cade asked.

The man looked at him and smiled, and Cade couldn't help but relax a bit. Instinct told him the guy was not going to hurt him. Still, he wouldn't let his guard down completely. He would be foolish to do that, especially considering his bizarre circumstances.

"Allow me to introduce myself," the man said, standing and extending his hand. "My name is Percy, and we have been assigned to work together."

Cade stood, dusting himself off while he tried to get his bearings, and shook the man's hand while quietly studying him. Percy was older, with graying hair, gray clothes, and gray skin. *Okay, that cannot be healthy. I think this guy needs a doctor.*

"I don't understand," Cade said. "Who assigned us to work together? How come I've never met you before?" He stopped, surprised at his questions. First, he needed to get to the bottom of what he was doing here. Everything else could come later, after he figured out why he wasn't dead. "Actually, I should ask you what the heck I was doing on the ground." *And why you were just sitting there, watching me,* he added silently.

Percy smiled. "I'm sure you have many questions, and I will be happy to answer them all. First, come sit beside me on the bench so we can talk. You have some processing to do."

Cade's head swam. His vision wasn't blurry, but his body was definitely off-balance. The feeling reminded him of being on a ship while the waves gently rolled beneath; he always had sense of working to remain steady on his feet.

"Processing? What's going on?"

Cade wasn't ready to sit on any bench. Whoever this guy was,

Cade needed answers. He knew from experience that he couldn't trust anyone, despite appearances. Percy might look like a nice old guy, but for all Cade knew he had dead bodies lined up in the crawl space under his house. "How about you just start talking?"

Percy nodded. "I know you don't trust easily, Cade, and this will be a difficult time for you. But I've been assigned to be your partner and help you through this."

"Partner? I don't work with partners." Cade was annoyed. His superiors knew that he worked alone. Detectives like him did not work with partners, and Cade wasn't about to start now. He'd spent ten years working as an undercover narcotics detective, and he knew what he was doing. He didn't want anyone else playing in the sandbox with him.

What the hell were they thinking? He was damn good at his job, and everyone in the police department knew it. He had a system, a way of working the streets, and he had developed liaisons and informants.

Wait… there was something… But as quickly as the memory came, it was gone, leaving him uncomfortable and disoriented.

"Remembering, Cade?" Percy asked.

The landscape shifted and the sky turned purple. The river heaved a sigh, causing the waters to swell and recede.

"What is this place?" Cade asked.

"Some people know this as the in-between, but I like to think of it as the void, a pause really, the place between life and death."

"What?" Cade was confused, but he couldn't let Percy see that. If this guy really was going to be his partner, he had to know that Cade could stand on his own and handle whatever was thrown at him. For now, Cade's main objective was to figure out what the hell was going on, which wasn't easy considering Percy's crazy answers.

Maybe he's not a cop, maybe he's just a weirdo.

"It's natural to be confused, and I think I'm going to add to your confusion," Percy said. "Let's start with the facts, as difficult as they may be."

Cade nodded. "Give it to me."

"Do you remember Eileen?" Percy asked.

"My informant," Cade answered. A single mom who got caught in a number of bad situations, or maybe just didn't know any better than to stay out of trouble, Eileen was always in the wrong place at the wrong time. Fortunately, she worked with Cade when he asked her. Of course he paid her for the information, but she had proved herself to be a reliable source, and he often turned to her for help.

That thought made him uncomfortable but he wasn't sure why. "What about her? Is she okay?"

"No, she's not," Percy said. "There's really no easy way to say this, so I'm just going to come out with it. Thaddeus Bruneux found out that Eileen was working with you."

"God, he had her killed, didn't he?" Cade knew Thaddeus, knew what a sonofabitch the guy could be. He was cold and ruthless and didn't care about anyone or anything. Word on the street was that he ran both prostitution and drugs, but nobody had been able to nail him on anything. Everyone was afraid of Thaddeus, even his own mother.

"I was working the case, getting what I needed to put him away for good," Cade muttered.

"He knew that, and he knew Eileen was feeding you information," Percy answered.

"Oh God, he's going to kill her." Cade had to do something to protect her, get her out of there. He couldn't let her die because of him.

"No, he turned it around on her." Percy's voice was gentle, prodding Cade toward an understanding of something. "Cade, this is never the easy part of this job, and believe me, I understand how difficult this moment is going to be for you. But I want you to close your eyes and think of the last thing that you can remember."

"Getting shot."

Percy nodded. "That was quick. I'm somewhat surprised that it didn't take you long."

Cade's laugh was humorless. "I woke up wondering if I was dead, so of course that's the first thing I remember. I suppose now you're going to tell me it's true, that I'm stuck here—" He waved his hand in the air, trying to figure out where he was. "Somewhere on the side of the river—"

"You're on the Colonial Parkway, to be exact," Percy interrupted. "But nobody knows you're here."

"Right, somewhere on the Colonial Parkway, so I can haunt the place, right?" Cade waited a moment, wondering if he was losing his mind.

"Um, close, but not exactly," Percy answered. "Come with me. Let's take a walk."

CHAPTER TWO

IF THIS IS DEAD, THEN what the hell was my life about? I tried to do the right thing…

But had he? Had he always done the right thing, or had he done what was easiest? An image of Eileen flashed through his mind.

I loved her. God help me, I loved her.

He never took a chance with that, though. He might have loved her, but it wasn't his place to do anything about it. She was his informant, and he was not about to cross that line. He wasn't that kind of guy.

But he'd wanted to, more times than he cared to admit, even to himself.

He remembered seeing her in the park last summer. She'd been wearing a bright blue sundress and for some reason that made him happy. Maybe he was happy because of her smile.

"You look nice," he told her.

She beamed up at him, her shyness at his compliment clear. "Thanks. I'm celebrating."

"Good news?"

She nodded. "I've been sober for a year, and I just got a phone call about that job I applied for last week. I'm going to be working at the dry cleaner's over on Mercury Boulevard."

"That's great," Cade said, wondering if it would be good for her to work with all those chemicals. "What about Jack?" Jack was her five-year-old son, a whirlwind of energy and cute as a button. Cade didn't usually like to hang out with kids, but Jack was charming, smart, and funny. He couldn't help but like the child.

"Jack is going to an all-day preschool now, so it's time for me to start putting my life back together," Eileen said. "I'm thinking about enrolling in college, too, but I don't know."

"College would be a good start," Cade said. "Is there something in particular you want to do when you grow up?" He winked as he said this, hoping to bring another smile to her face.

Instead of smiling, she grew serious. "I'd like to do something where I can give back," she said. "I keep thinking there are so many people out there who helped me when I really needed it, and I probably wouldn't be here today if it wasn't for all of you. I want to do something to help others, but I'm not sure what that will be."

Cade nodded. The truth was, Eileen had been a mess. She was an addict, and when he met her she was just hitting her bottom. Jack had been removed from her home by social services and was living in foster care. She was way too skinny from not eating, and she had a cough that wouldn't quit. The first time he'd spoken to her she'd actually snarled at him like a trapped animal.

Eventually she'd learned to trust Cade, and gradually she felt safe in feeding him information when he asked. She knew people who were still using, and she heard and saw all sorts of things in her neighborhood. He never knew if she acted as his informant out of a sense of guilt, misguided responsibility, or a desire to make a little extra cash. He always assumed it was a combination of all three things.

But that day, in her dress, with the sunlight bringing out the red highlights in her dark hair, he thought she'd never looked more lovely. *Maybe it's the enthusiasm for starting over, the realization that she's really got a shot at a different life.*

A better life.

He wanted that for Eileen and Jack, he wanted them to have a happy-ever-after sort of life. She wasn't a bad person, she'd just gotten a little lost along the way.

"I'm sure whatever you decide to do will make the world a better place," he said, meaning every word.

"Thanks. I really appreciate that, and everything you've done for me," she answered, smiling shyly at him.

That was a good day, and there had been other good days with her. Other times they had laughed together or shared a meal or a joke. Cade never went to see Eileen without bringing something for Jack, too, some sort of toy or book. The kid loved to read, and Cade had spent much of his time with Eileen reading stories to Jack. Times like that left Cade wondering what it would have been like to have kids of his own.

Cade had been married once, a long time ago, but like so many who worked undercover the relationship didn't last. How could it? The late nights, the erratic schedule, the constant worry about whether or not he would be killed…

Janie knew I'd get myself killed eventually. I can't blame her for leaving.

He didn't want that for Eileen. He wanted her to have a chance at normalcy, with a man who would be sure to come home at night after work. Cade didn't usually get home until early morning, and he didn't want his work spilling into his life.

Best to leave Eileen alone, let her get on with her plans. She made it out of a dark place, she deserves the best.

Percy interrupted his thoughts. "You let yourself get cynical."

"I didn't let myself get cynical, the reality of the world made it happen." Cade was annoyed. Who the hell was this guy to tell him how he should feel? Of course he was cynical, how could he not be? He'd been on the front lines of the worst of humanity every stinking day of his life.

"People aren't that bad, you know," Percy said.

"Maybe on this side of the afterlife they're not," Cade answered. "But trust me, earth breeds the worst of the worst." If he was dead and stuck in some kind of limbo because of his attitude, then fine. He couldn't help how he felt, especially after seeing the crap he'd seen in his decade on the job.

"You seem to have accepted your situation already," Percy said.

Cade shrugged. The truth was he hadn't. He didn't really believe he was dead, since everything looked and felt the same. For crying out loud, he was in a car. Dead people didn't ride in cars.

"Are you hungry?" Percy asked.

"No, not really." Cade was surprised. Usually he had a voracious appetite and loved to snack. "Is that part of being dead?" *That would stink if I couldn't eat again.* Of all the things he thought he would miss when he died, food hadn't occurred to him. But the thought of never again tasting a steak grilled to perfection, or strawberry cheesecake, or bacon, filled him with remorse.

"You will be, it just takes time," Percy said. "It isn't the same, though. When you eat, as with everything else you do now, you'll feel slightly removed."

"What does that mean?"

"I mean that when you touch something, or eat something, you'll feel as if you're not getting the entire experience. The colors around you are a bit more muted, and the food won't quite taste the same. Warm and cold don't bother us at all, and we don't usually smell things unless they are truly odiferous."

"Because we're dead."

Percy nodded. "Yes, because we're dead. But this state of being has perks, too." Percy pulled the car into a turn-off that was meant to give tourists a dazzling view. Gulls were circling overhead, and dark clouds were still rolling across the sky. "Watch."

Again, Cade couldn't help but wonder if he was making a good choice. What if he was dead but stuck with some sort of mentally ill angel? That would be just perfect, an eternity with a deranged soul who probably had a supply of meds that wouldn't work.

"You have quite the imagination," Percy said, smiling.

Cade squirmed. "Can you read my mind, too?"

"No, but I can see you processing all sorts of thoughts about who I am and what I'm capable of," Percy answered. "I promise, I will not hurt you."

And with that, Percy pulled out a pocketknife and drove it into Cade's neck.

CHAPTER THREE

CADE WAS SERIOUSLY PISSED. "ALL I'm saying is a little warning would have been nice."

"I suppose, but I was trying to make a point."

"You could've just told me," Cade said. "You didn't have to scare the crap out of me."

"The element of surprise made it more fun," Percy said. "Plus, you wouldn't have believed me, and I would have had to stab you anyway."

Cade shook his head, still taken aback by the fact of his non-injury. Apparently being dead had some perks, as it looked like he couldn't be seriously injured. But the fact was that he remained dead, and that was a fairly permanent state of being. Sorrow began to take hold of him, seeping into his body, a body that could not bleed.

He would never marry again.

He would never have children.

He would never know a simple, peaceful retirement.

He would never kiss Eileen.

So, what the hell am I doing here?

"What next?" he asked.

Percy looked at him for a long moment. "Burying your feelings will not help you survive this, you know."

Cade blew out a breath. "I know, but there's no way for me to handle this right now. I'm dead, I get it, but I'm not in heaven and I'm not in hell, I'm sitting here with you. So what are we supposed to do? Haunt the place? Scare people?"

"Goodness, no, not at all," Percy said. "As I mentioned earlier, we have an assignment. Basically, we are here only when we have a mission. We don't always get to live here on earth unless we have a long term assignment."

"This is all starting to sound like some kind of military thing," Cade muttered. "Okay, so what happens when we complete our assignment? Do we get graded?"

Percy shook his head. "No, it's not quite like that. You see, we all take our turn on the wheel. You've heard of karma, right?"

"Sort of," Cade said. "What comes around goes around, something like that."

"Karma dictates our lifetimes," Percy said. "If, for example, you lived a life of being unkind to everyone around you, then your next turn on the wheel would be spent experiencing the negativity that you created."

"We get more than one life?" Cade was stunned. He had always dismissed past lives as something that was made up, not real. "How many lives do we get?"

Percy laughed. "We don't get a set number of lifetimes, we simply choose to keep returning until we get it right and we can then move on to a higher level of existence. But there are those, like us, who didn't quite get it right, but we didn't quite get it wrong. We spent our lifetimes indifferent, lived without caring, days slipping by without purpose."

Cade exploded. "What kind of crap is that? I dedicated my life to helping others, to cleaning up the streets, to taking care of people who were in trouble. When a call came, I went. I spent time on the SWAT team, for crissakes, I was one of those guys who stormed into buildings and put my life on the line to save everyone else from an active shooter."

Percy leveled a look at him. "Did you love?"

"Did I love what?"

"Did you love the people you protected, or did you just do your job because it was a job? Did all the filth and poverty and hatred that you saw fill you with an emptiness so vast that you found yourself living within that void?"

Cade didn't answer. He didn't want to have this conversation. "Let's get on with this. What are we supposed to be doing?"

Percy stared at him for a moment, silent. "You'll have to give it some thought later. You can't run away from why you're here."

Cade sighed, clearly ready to let go of the whole subject. "Our assignment?"

"Okay, our assignment is to help a young mother who has nothing for Christmas. She is on welfare, but there won't be enough—"

"Drugs?" Cade interrupted. At Percy's blank stare, he asked again. "Is this young mother using?"

Percy nodded. "Yes, but—"

"How long has she been in the system?"

"Her name is Michelle Baxter, she's been on welfare most of her life, addicted to a variety of substances and in and out of jail on several prostitution charges. Her family has had a number of run-ins with police, but all of them are now dead, and she is alone. Her son is ten years old and very smart, gets all As in school."

"I've seen this before. She uses everything in the system,

generations of her family stuck on welfare. Getting welfare or benefits from others is her job, right? She doesn't actually work, has no intention of working. So now what you're telling me is that she gets to take advantage of services on earth as well as from the great beyond? Seriously?"

Cade was pissed. He knew her type, he knew what she was all about. *I wonder if I can request a transfer.* He grimaced, realizing where he might end up.

"Give this a try." Percy's voice was gentle. "Remember, you're carrying lifetimes of old resentments and horror at the state of humanity. You have spent many years in law enforcement, living in various places around the world, and you've seen a lot. Perhaps you've seen too much."

"Are you talking about my other lives?" Cade asked. *Where the hell have I lived?*

"Yes, but let's not get distracted. Our assignment lives in Gloucester, a lovely little county."

"I know where Gloucester is," Cade muttered. "I grew up in Hampton Roads." Gloucester was a rural county north of Yorktown, a small community known for hosting a daffodil festival each year. Like every other place on earth, it had a dark underbelly that people rarely acknowledged. He did not want to do this, but apparently his assignment came from the very high-up. "Okay, give me the address and I'll meet you there later."

Percy hesitated. "Cade, you're supposed to stay with me so I can help you through this. We work together as a team."

"Yeah, sure, I just need a little time alone first," Cade said. "I am kind of new to being dead, you know."

"Okay, meet me in the Gloucester Courthouse area around dinner time. We can do what needs to be done then, and I'll show you how it works."

Cade started to walk away, and Percy called after him. "One more thing, Cade. Just so you know, we don't have any special powers. You're going to have to walk to wherever you want to go."

73

CHAPTER FOUR

MAYBE BECAUSE PERCY WAS A being from the great beyond he would know what Cade was up to, but Cade didn't care. His only thought was to find Eileen.

But it would have been nice if I didn't have to walk.

Percy said that this had happened because of Thaddeus. He needed to make sure she and Jack were not hurt. He couldn't bear to imagine what that scumbag might have done to them.

Cade covered the distance to Eileen's apartment in less time than he expected. *Maybe I'm walking faster*, he thought. *Or I've got some kind of ability to move differently.*

He stood on the cracked pavement outside the square brick building, looking up at the third floor where he knew she lived. He imagined she was in there, maybe doing dishes at the kitchen sink with the leaky faucet, or picking up toys that were scattered through Jack's room, or folding up the pull-out couch where she slept. As a single mother, Eileen could not afford more than a one-bedroom apartment, and she made sure that Jack got the bedroom for himself.

Or maybe she wasn't in there at all. Maybe she too was dead.

"Excuse me." When he turned around, Cade saw a woman holding a grocery bag in her arms that partially obscured her face.

"Sorry, ma'am," he said.

The woman muttered something and moved past him, edging toward the front door with the broken lock. *There never was any security here. Anyone could walk in at any time.*

Something about the way she walked caught Cade's attention. "Eileen?"

The woman slowly turned and faced him, looking resigned to whatever he had to say to her. When she lifted her head to him, he saw the yellowish-purple of fading bruises.

"What happened?" He started to reach out to her, but stopped when a look of fear crossed her face. "Are you okay?" He looked her up and down, wondering if she was bruised anywhere else and how badly she was hurt. *Son of a bitch, Thaddeus did this. I know it.*

She didn't speak for a moment, but stood as if she were frozen in place. "Excuse me?" she asked.

"Eileen, I know about Thaddeus, I won't let him hurt you again."

Fear and shame washed across her face as she backed away from him. "I'm sorry, I don't think I know you," she said. "And I don't know how you—"

"Is Jack hurt, too?" Cade interrupted. He couldn't stand the thought of that innocent kid getting hurt because of a scumbag like Thaddeus.

"How do you know my son?"

Cade stopped, unsure of himself. *She really doesn't know who I am. She's not faking this.* He still didn't understand how this whole being-dead-and-on-assignment thing was supposed to work, but it made sense that she wouldn't know who he was. His years of undercover training kicked in, and he blurted out the first thing he could think of. "I… heard about it down at the station. Everyone's hoping you're okay."

Her shoulders relaxed marginally, so Cade kept talking, hoping to win her trust. Clearly she didn't recognize him, which he hadn't expected, but maybe he could still help her. *Screw that woman in Gloucester, this is who I need to help.* "I told Sergeant Marcucci that I would stop by and see how you were doing, but he never told me the whole story about what happened. I only know the bits and pieces the other guys are talking about."

She spoke so softly he had to lean forward to catch her words. "The newspaper got it all wrong, but maybe that's for the best."

Cade nodded, playing along. Of course something about his death would have been in the newspaper, he hadn't thought of that. "The media screws everything up."

"Good thing," Eileen said. She finally looked directly at him. "Is everyone mad at me?"

"No," Cade answered. "Everyone knows what Thaddeus is. Why don't we sit over here and talk for a minute?" He gestured to a bench on a sparse patch of grass, a place where they had spent many hours sitting and talking about everything from information Cade needed to Jack losing his first tooth.

Cade wondered if sitting with him in that spot would cause Eileen to recognize him.

"I don't understand why they put that stuff in the newspaper, though," Eileen said. "I understand that they are probably still investigating, but why would they say that Cade was killed interrupting a crime?"

Cade thought for a moment. He wasn't sure what the official statement had been, and he was still sorting out the series of events himself. "So, have you read anything about them arresting someone?" He wondered if he could get Eileen to fill in some of the gaps for him.

She sniffled and tears spilled down her cheeks. "The investigation is… ongoing. That's what they told me at the funeral yesterday." She looked up at him, her eyes huge. "Did I meet you there?"

Cade shook his head. "I've been sort of in and out of places." He left his statement purposefully vague, knowing full well she wouldn't figure out that he hadn't been there.

"I knew that there would be a lot of officers, but that was the first funeral I've been to for…" She stopped talking, and her hand rose to her throat. "I'm sorry, you must think I'm an idiot."

"I know that you worked with him," Cade said softly. "Cade talked about you all the time." He felt weird speaking about himself in the third person but clearly he had no choice.

"He died because of me, you know," Eileen said, her voice flat. "He died because I'm not strong enough."

"Cade's death is not your fault," he said. Of all the things he'd expected to hear from her, a confession was not it.

"I told the police—your co-workers, I guess. I told them all about it, then I started packing. But they said I couldn't leave town." She started crying in earnest then, and he wasn't sure what to do. Reaching out, he stroked her back, hoping she could feel his touch but not sure what he would do if she couldn't.

After a few minutes of sobbing into her hands, Eileen sat up and wiped her face. Taking a breath, she looked directly at Cade. "You must think I'm incredibly selfish. Maybe I am. All I really know is that right now I'm very confused."

"Why don't you talk about it? It will help to get it all out," he said. *Good God, how the hell did I die? I don't remember it too clearly, but I know Eileen was not there.*

"They came to see me a couple of weeks ago," Eileen said. "Thaddeus and his thugs." She paused for a moment and began shaking her head, arms wrapped around her middle. "I probably shouldn't say this, but I hate them."

Cade thought about karma and what Percy had said. "Hate's a pretty strong emotion. You might want to try to let go of some of that." Of course he couldn't really tell her why he said that, could he? He imagined it would be a bit of a surprise for him to say, *Oh, yeah, I'm Cade but you don't recognize me and I'm actually dead but still sort of alive so I can finish some project here.* That sort of thing didn't usually go over well with people.

Looking directly at him, Eileen said, "They told me that if I didn't tell them who I worked for they were going to kill my baby. They had a knife to my son's throat."

A flash of gratitude struck Cade. Thank God they didn't hurt Jack. Wait—that's not what she said. "They didn't hurt Jack, did they?" As soon as the words left his mouth he realized his mistake, but fortunately Eileen didn't ask again how Cade knew her son's name.

"No, they actually let him go. I thought we were both going to die that night, but Thaddeus told me I was a good little girl and to get ready for his next assignment." Tears welled up in her eyes again. "He told me I worked for him now."

Cade thought for a moment, trying to piece together the timeline in his mind. "So, after they threatened you, they must have sent Ronnie out to do the job. Did they hold you hostage?"

Eileen nodded. "Yes, I told the police this when I made my statement. They had been in my kitchen, waiting for us. After I told them what they wanted to hear, they tied us to the kitchen chairs, and we waited. It felt like hours, but I don't think it was that long before Thaddeus got a phone call."

Cade nodded. "Ronnie did it. He pulled the trigger."

Eileen's eyes lit up. "Does that mean you're going to make an arrest? Is it safe for Jack to come home now?"

"No, it is not safe, and no, there will be no arrest. You and Jack are being taken someplace out of state for your own protection."

"As a matter of fact—"

Cade turned around to see who was talking, but he knew before he even set eyes on the man. "What are you doing here?" Cade asked. *He has somehow managed to make himself look like an undercover cop*, Cade thought, taking in Percy's jeans and rumpled shirt. *Unbelievable.*

"Same as you," Percy said. "Consoling the bereaved."

Confusion crossed Eileen's face. "Do you guys work together?" She was standing and looked like she was ready to run at any second. "Is something going on here?"

Cade reached a hand out to her, wanting to make a connection. "No—I mean yes, we work together, but no, there's nothing going on."

"I came here to get my co-worker so we could follow up on a possible lead," Percy said. "But for the time being, you need to get inside your apartment and start packing a suitcase. Sergeant Marcucci will be here in thirty minutes to pick you up. Your son is safe, and the two of you will be going somewhere else to start a new life."

"Kind of like a witness protection thing?" Eileen asked, doubt lacing her voice.

"That is exactly what this is," Percy answered.

Eileen stood, staring at Percy and Cade. After a moment, Cade spoke. "She probably doesn't have a suitcase; we should get one for her."

Percy looked at Cade and smiled. "Thank you for reminding me. I'll be right back." When Percy walked to a car and opened the door, Cade fumed. *Not able to drive, huh? How come he gets a car, and I had to walk here?*

Reaching into the trunk, Percy pulled out a black suitcase with wheels and brought it to where Eileen stood. "Compliments of the force," he said, smiling. Percy leaned over, hugged her and stepped back, leaving his hands on her shoulders. "You and your son are going to be fine. You didn't do anything wrong, and I'm sure if Cade were here he would tell you that, too. Cade loved you, and he loved your son. He would have been glad to know that he died instead of you."

That's true. There's no way I would have been able to live with myself if Eileen and Jack had gotten hurt trying to protect me.

Percy turned to Cade. "We need to go. We have that other assignment we need to be working on, and we don't have much time."

"I'm sorry," Eileen said. "I hope I haven't made you late for anything."

"No," Cade said. His emotions were jumbled as he stared at her. *This might be the last time I see her.* "I'm glad you're going to be okay. And… Percy's right. Cade wouldn't have wanted you to get hurt."

He couldn't stand to look at her any longer, knowing what he'd lost. In his time with her, Cade had had plenty of opportunities to come clean and confess his feelings. He hadn't done anything, and that lost chance for a real love would be a burden he carried to the grave.

Literally.

CHAPTER FIVE

"STOP POUTING. IT'S NOT A very attractive look on a police officer," Percy said.

"Detective. I'm a detective," Cade snapped. "And the fact remains that you lied to me. I don't appreciate that."

"I didn't lie, all I said was that you were going to have to walk. I told you the truth."

"You could've let me use the car," Cade said.

"Why would I let you use my car?"

"Because it's the polite thing to do."

"But it's my car," Percy argued. "Why should I just hand over the keys to the new guy?"

"Aren't you supposed to be all about non-attachment to material things?" Cade asked.

"No, that's the Buddhists."

Cade covered his face with his hands, not sure he wanted to have this conversation anymore. *Maybe I'm in a coma, and this is all part of some delirious state I'm in. This can't be real.*

"So now that you've tried to work things out with the girl who got away, are you going to settle down and do what you've been asked to do?" Percy interrupted his thoughts.

"Do I have a choice?" Cade said.

"We always have a choice," Percy answered.

But Cade knew better than most that sometimes having choices didn't mean much. *It just means you get to choose between crappy and super-crappy. Like the time I had to bust the department store Santa for selling crack in the mall parking lot.* Sure enough, small children had seen Cade shoving Santa into a police cruiser, but unfortunately he couldn't tell them why he had to do it.

Certainly not one of his best days.

"So, partner, what do we do now?"

"I'm going to ignore your sarcastic tone and get on with this project," Percy said, staring at the road. "I've already given you enough information about the subject, now I'm going to set you up to do your thing."

"What thing?"

"Don't worry; you'll know what to do."

"What if I don't? I'm not used to getting sent into a situation without instructions," Cade argued. "Please tell me the fate of the world does not depend on this."

"The fate of the world depends on other things," Percy said. "You have nothing to fear. All you are being asked to do is try."

It's not like I have anything else to do.

* * *

As part of the Chesapeake Bay region of Virginia, Gloucester was bordered mostly by water, including the York River, Mobjack Bay, and Ware River. Like most counties of this type in Virginia, Gloucester had a large share of farmers and fishermen, most of them carrying on a family tradition. The land was flat, bisected by Route 17, a four-lane road that meandered from Florida all the way up through northern Virginia.

Cade was never really sure how he felt about Gloucester. Like most rural areas, the county had a mixed economic population, from the generations of poverty-stricken families to the wealthy newcomers who purchased waterfront property. Gloucester Courthouse was his favorite place, though; an historic area that was settled in 1651, the courthouse buildings and small green were almost reminiscent of an old New England town.

But he still got a sense of uneasiness in Gloucester, and he wasn't sure if that was because he knew too much. He'd worked there for a while, and he knew the ways that people hid their meth labs in all this farmland, he knew that kids got locked in cages in the trailer parks, and he knew how some families carried their shameful secrets of abuse, refusing to believe there was any other way to live.

What the hell kind of good could he do in the midst of all that?

Percy turned into a parking lot and pulled into a space. He reached into the storage compartment in the middle of the car and pulled out a slightly crumpled folder. "This is a picture of your subject," Percy said, trying to smooth out the photo. "You'll see her in the grocery store when you go in. When you get out of the car, go into the store, pick up some bananas and get in line at the checkout."

Cade nodded and waited. The silence stretched between them. "And?" he prompted.

"Just go," Percy said. "Go now, you're running out of time."

Bananas. He hated bananas, but maybe Percy would eat the damn things.

A display of holiday wreaths and Christmas trees were stacked outside the sliding double doors. *I don't think I even put up a tree this year*, Cade thought. *Actually, I can't remember the last time I put up a tree. No real reason for it.*

Jazzy Christmas carols played throughout the store, and fake presents were stacked next to a cookie display. He walked to the produce section and began looking at the fruit. *What if I pick the wrong bananas? Am I supposed to get a certain kind?* A more important thought jolted through him. *Do I have any money? How am I supposed to pay for this?*

Knowing he had no real choice but to trust Percy, Cade grabbed a bunch of bananas and went to the cash register. He stood for a moment, assessing his options. Then he saw her, standing at register six. Cade walked to the line and stood behind Michelle Baxter, the woman he had been assigned to.

Michelle was talking on her phone and he could hear every word she said. He shamelessly eavesdropped. "I'm telling you, that dickwad better come up with the money he owes me or he's gonna be getting some serious you-know-what coming his way. I'm not waitin no more for him." Cade couldn't make out what the person on the other end of the phone was saying, but wasn't sure he wanted to know anyway.

Michelle kept talking as the cashier rang up her purchases. "Yeah, I know, right?"

I wonder if she's going to stay on the phone while she pays.

"That'll be twenty dollars and fifty-two cents," the cashier said.

Michelle didn't even look at her, she just pulled a small credit card out of her pocket and said, "I got my EBT card." Cade knew that meant she was on food stamps, and wondered again what he was supposed to be doing.

"I'm sorry ma'am, your card has been denied," the cashier said.

Finally, Michelle paid attention. "I gotta go, they're telling me my card don't work." Ending the call, she looked at the cashier. "That can't be right, I know I got money on there. I'm owed some food, you know."

"You can try to run it through again," the cashier said. "Maybe the card reader made an error."

"Yeah, that's probably what happened," Michelle muttered.

Michelle ran the card through the machine again, and the cashier shook her head. "I'm sorry ma'am, it still says that it doesn't work. Maybe you should try calling the main number to see what the problem is."

"I know what the problem is," Michelle snarled. "The problem is those idiots in Washington who don't want my kid to have any food, that's the problem. They've all got their heads stuck up their—"

"I'll have someone put the food back for you," the cashier interrupted, deftly moving the bags of groceries to an area under the cash register. Michelle walked out, muttering and shaking her head at the indignities that she had just suffered.

She thinks the whole world owes her a free ride.

Cade looked at the cashier who smiled up at him. "Good afternoon, sir," she chirped. The kid couldn't have been more than eighteen years old, yet she carried herself with more grace than many adults Cade knew. She had certainly handled that situation well.

"Do you know her?" he asked.

The cashier nodded. "Yeah, she always has problems with that card. She should get a new one."

"Huh," Cade said. He left his bananas on the conveyor belt and walked out of the store.

CHAPTER SIX

"WHERE'S MY BANANAS?" PERCY ASKED as Cade climbed into the car.

"I saw Michelle," Cade said. "What a piece of work."

Percy stared out the window for a moment before asking, "What happened in there, Cade?"

"I grabbed the bananas, just like you said, then I saw her standing in line with a bunch of groceries so I went and stood behind her. She was yapping on her cell phone most of the time, but when her food stamp card didn't work she got off the phone."

Cade shook his head. Some people truly needed the help they got from sources such as the food stamp program or soup kitchens. He wasn't sure about Michelle, though; she looked to him like another user who took advantage of anything she could get her hands on.

"What did you do when her card didn't work?" Percy asked.

Cade shrugged. "I watched. She got annoyed and stormed out.

Why, was I supposed to do something?"

Percy didn't say anything, he just stared out the window at the expanse of pavement. Finally, he smiled. "I suppose the good news is that there are always chances to redeem ourselves. You'll just have to try again."

Cade was puzzled. "But I don't know what I'm supposed to do. Am I watching her? Am I interacting with her? What?"

"Eventually you'll get it," Percy said. "You just have to let your true self out of the cage you've built."

"My true self?"

"The part of you that is connected to the Divine," Percy explained. "That is the part of you that knows the answers to most of the hardest questions. Sometimes we simply need to learn how to access that part. Now, I want you to go back into the store."

"But Michelle is long gone, I saw her get into a car and leave," Cade said.

"I know that. But I wanted some bananas."

* * *

Cade wasn't sure he really would know what to do. *I'm not very good at this*, he thought. *No wonder I'm stuck in the in-between.*

He was sitting with Percy at an outside table in front of Olivia's restaurant on Main Street. The mild December day had attracted a large number of shoppers to the area, and a sense of excitement was in the air. Christmas was only four days away.

"So, are there angels with harps and things?" he asked. Maybe if he could get a handle on the hierarchy, he might know better what to do.

"Every imaginable thing in the universe exists," Percy said. "And there are some creatures that humans have yet to imagine."

"That sounds a little scary," Cade said. "Are we talking demons or are we talking something else?"

Percy shook his head. "I don't mean for it to be scary. But there are levels of existence on many different dimensions, and there are creatures who fit each dimension. But you'll learn about this gradually, and none of it affects you right now."

Cade was silent for a moment. *Now what? I've adjusted to being dead, but I've got to complete this assignment that so far I have completely failed.* Being dead was nothing like he'd expected. His body was still solid, but he didn't bleed or get hurt. True, he had a bit of the same gray tinge that Percy had, but he didn't think he was as gray as his partner. He was pretty sure he still looked the same, but people didn't recognize him, which was probably a good thing. Most of the time he wasn't hungry or tired. In fact, the only time he was tired was when he thought about Eileen or tried to figure out what the heck he was supposed to do.

He wasn't sure what he was doing wrong, but every time he saw Michelle he was not able to get anything done. At least, nothing that Percy approved of.

Clearly he was supposed to have done something in the grocery store, but he wasn't sure what. Then, later that day, Percy put him in Michelle's path again. Michelle and her son were in a car that was stuck on the side of the road.

"They're having car problems," Percy said. "Go see them."

Cade had gone to check on things, but the owner of the car told him that a tow truck was on the way, not to worry. "Is everyone okay?" he'd asked.

"Sure, these are my friends, we'll be fine," the man had answered. Cade didn't see any real problem or distress, and the tow truck had arrived.

Looks like they have a ride to wherever they're going, he thought, walking back to his partner. Percy was waiting for him and didn't speak for a few minutes after Cade got back into his car.

"So, what did you think?" Percy finally asked.

"I think you'd better give me more guidelines or something,

because I don't know what you expect of me," Cade said. "She and the kid were fine; the tow truck showed up, what was I supposed to do?"

"Next time, all you have to do is listen to the quiet voice within," Percy said. "If I tell you what to do it's not the same as you knowing what to do."

The sound of a bell ringing focused Cade's attention again. Percy was now standing and reaching into his coat pocket. He handed Cade the car keys.

"Have fun, cowboy," Percy said.

"What, I've finally reached the rank of being able to drive your car?"

"No, this is still part of your assignment. Take the car and go for a drive," Percy said. Looking up at the sky, he added, "I have an umbrella in the backseat. Rain's coming." Smiling at Cade, he gave a little wave and walked away. In a matter of seconds, Percy had disappeared into the crowd.

How did he do that?

Shaking his head, Cade stood and put some money on the table for their coffee. He walked to the older model Camry that Percy drove, got in, and stared out the windshield. Percy's words came back to him. *Listen to the quiet voice within.*

After a moment, he started the car and pulled out. He didn't think about where he was driving, he just let himself go on autopilot and began driving down Main Street, out of the courthouse area. As he drove, the sky above him darkened and thunder rumbled in the distance. He turned the headlights on, knowing it was only a matter of minutes before the rain hit.

He was turning left onto Route 17 when the torrential downpour began. His visibility was diminished and he had to slow down to a crawl. *I can barely see in front of me. I wonder what happens when dead people crash a car.*

After five minutes of driving through the rain, hands gripping the wheel, he noticed something on the side of the road ahead of him. *Looks like someone got caught in the rain.*

He shook his head, knowing this was not the kind of weather anyone needed to be out in. Pulling closer to the person walking on the side of the road, he saw that it was actually two people. He pushed the button to lower the side window. "Do you want a ride?" He had to yell to be heard over the pounding of the rain. They nodded and came to the car, opening the door and climbing in.

He wasn't even a little bit surprised to see that it was Michelle and a young boy.

CHAPTER SEVEN

"SO THAT'S IT, ALL I had to do was give them a ride?" Cade was dubious. The whole thing seemed way too simple.

"No, because that's not all you did," Percy said. "You showed them kindness."

Cade stared out at the York River. They were in the same spot as when he'd first woken up and discovered he was dead. "So I was supposed to show them kindness each time I saw them? That's it?" Cade was incredulous. "There's got to be more to this than that."

Percy shook his head. "There really isn't. The first time you met Michelle was in the grocery store, right?"

"Right."

"She couldn't purchase her food because of a glitch, right?"

Understanding dawned. "I was supposed to pay for her food," Cade said.

Percy smiled. "Yes. Unfortunately, her son paid the price for that, as he didn't have any food in the house that day."

Regret pierced Cade. He would never willingly let a kid go hungry.

"The child is fine," Percy said softly. "He has been taken care of."

"And that time they were in the car, waiting for the tow truck? Was I supposed to give them a ride?"

"Yes. The purpose of that was to show the child that there is kindness in this world, and nothing is completely hopeless."

I used to think that wasn't true. Maybe there is always some sort of hope.

Images of the cruelties he'd witnessed time and time again flashed through his mind: the young woman, beaten by her pimp until she could no longer speak; the eight-year-old girl weighing thirty pounds because her parents never fed her; the elderly man lying in a pool of his own blood after being attacked and beaten.

But around those images others seeped in, too, images of the people he loved, the simple joy of being on a boat, fishing. Images of all the Christmases he had spent as a child, waiting for the magic to happen. His parents always made the holidays full of love, warmth, and magic for the whole family.

"I want to show you something," Percy said. "Look out at the river."

Cade stared at the water, which had begun to darken and roll. As he did so, he saw an image of a young boy. He squinted, staring at the boy, who appeared to be bagging groceries.

"Michelle's son," he whispered.

"Hush," Percy said. "Pay attention."

The boy was cheerful and full of warmth, smiling at every customer and working hard to do a good job. A balding, middle-aged man stepped up to the conveyor belt, waiting to pay for his food.

"Hello sir, and Merry Christmas," the boy said. "My name is Hank. Do you need help bringing this out to your car?"

The man scowled at Hank. "No."

"Are you okay?" Hank asked. The customer didn't answer, just

stared at the ceiling, waiting for his food. Hank reached a hand out and touched the man's arm. "Sometimes things seem really hopeless, especially around this time of year. But I learned when I was just a kid that there is kindness out there, and there are lots of people who care. Really care. Whatever it is, hang on, because it does get better. Sometimes it just takes a little time."

The man stared at Hank for a long moment, then finally nodded, picked up his bags, and left.

"He turned into a pretty decent kid," Cade said. "Michelle should be proud of him."

"He always had the capacity to be a caring soul," Percy said. "Your actions showed him that people do care. When you gave them a ride that day and treated them with respect it gave young Hank the encouragement he needed to believe that everything would work out."

"So now he's nice to others," Cade said.

"Yes, but there's more to it than that. The man that you saw him speaking to? That man was planning on going home and blowing his brains out. He was buying food as one last act for his wife and child."

Cade was chilled. "He had a kid?"

"An infant, actually. The child would have grown up without both parents, as the mother would not have made it in this world without the father and she would have died an early death. But Hank's simple and sincere words changed the course of events for that entire family."

"Hank gave him hope," Cade said. Could it really be that simple?

"When we help people, we never know who we are truly helping," Percy said. "We are all connected, and when we pull out one thread of the fabric there is the potential of having it all unravel."

"Hard to know if we're always doing the right thing," Cade

said. "We just don't know."

"It's best that way—the not knowing. If humans knew what aspect of the future they were affecting, the consequences could be devastating."

Cade ran a hand through his hair. "Now what?"

Percy smiled. "Now, we celebrate Christmas. Your body might no longer exist in the way it used to, but you're still here. Your essence, your spirit, that's the part that lives on so you can continue to learn and grow and do the work you were meant to do."

"I guess that's my Christmas present," Cade said. "Looks like I get a life for Christmas. It might not be what I'm used to, but still…"

"You've got a life," Percy agreed.

CHAPTER EIGHT

THE SCENE WAS AS IT had been since time was born from the void. The strains of a soft melody hung in the air as the last of the holiday workers filed into the clearing. The faint light of dawn was waking into the space, revealing row after row of the gray people. Some could barely be seen as their image shimmered in the soft light. Excitement hung in the air at the possibilities of this post-Christmas meeting.

Cade didn't know what to expect and stayed close to Percy. He tried to count the number of others that had gathered, but he couldn't. There were too many, and he couldn't see all the individuals.

He leaned in to whisper to Percy. "Am I supposed to do anything?"

"Gabe will lead the meeting," Percy said. "He usually asks about our assignments and gives us a chance to talk."

Cade sat in stunned silence, trying to absorb his new situation.

Everything had happened very quickly, and he was still somewhat surprised to find himself dead.

Yet, he lived on. When he was alive he hadn't given the whole afterlife thing much thought. Sure, he'd gone to church as a kid and had taken a World Religions class in college once. But even though his career held an element of danger, he'd never really believed he would die young.

Nobody wants to believe that's going to happen to them.

In his wildest imaginings, he would never have thought of the universe as so vast, so full of other kinds of life.

"Hello everyone, I'm Gabe." Gabe's voice was clear and rich, reminding Cade of a well-tuned instrument. "I know many of you are new to our group, and I want to tell you how excited I am about that. This is the place of second chances, where the mystery of the Grace holds a possibility for each of you to heal your brokenness and return to being whole."

Cade listened, fascinated, as Gabe invited those present to talk about their recent experiences. Some were still confused, not sure why they were there. Others, like Percy, had been doing this type of work for a while and chose to continue rather than move on. *Kind of like guardian angels*, Cade thought.

Cade brought his attention back to what Gabe was saying. "So, as you can see we've had plenty of new additions and lots of different experiences. I'm very interested to hear from one of our new members, Cade. He comes to us with an extensive background in law enforcement, not just in this lifetime but others as well. Cade, would you like to tell us about your assignment?"

Not really, but I don't think I have much of a choice here.

"Sure," he stood and addressed Gabe. "I have to tell you, I'm still a little nervous and kind of getting used to this whole in-between existence. I wasn't very good at the job you gave me, and it took me a long time to get this thing right. In fact, I don't think I could have done it without Percy and his encouragement."

Percy smiled back at him and winked.

"When I was alive, I never thought about how we are all connected. Of course I was careful when I made an arrest and a kid was there—I would always try to keep things peaceful for the kid's sake. Depending on the situation, I might have even put my weapon away. But I never thought beyond the immediate, or into the future. It never occurred to me."

Cade wondered if the others knew he was nervous. He hated talking in front of crowds, and the fact that he was talking to a bunch of dead people did nothing to ease his anxiety.

"So, I guess this whole thing is kind of like undercover work. Nobody really knows who we are, and we're trying to make things better for everyone. That's the way I used to approach my job. I guess I wanted to say thank you for this opportunity, too, because without it I'm not sure where I'd be." A round of nervous laughter erupted, and Cade knew everyone there must have had the same thought.

"Cade, we are honored to work with you," Gabe said. "You are bringing to us a world of experience that is invaluable."

"Thank you, sir," Cade said, wondering if he was addressing Gabe properly. *What is this guy's title, anyway? Sir angel? Sir archangel? Angel Sergeant?* "I'm looking forward to my next assignment."

As scattered applause erupted, Cade sat again. *How long will I have regrets about losing Eileen? How long will I have regrets about how I lived my life?*

Percy leaned over and said, "You did great, Cade. All the other things you're feeling will work out eventually, but it may take time. With each assignment you will learn more and grow more until you are ready to move on the next part of your evolution."

"Thanks. I can't help but wonder about everyone I've left behind, though. Is Eileen going to be okay? Are they going to arrest Ronnie for killing me? What about my friends and the little family I have?"

"Do you remember me telling you about the wheel when I first met you?" Percy asked. Cade nodded, and Percy continued. "We all get on and off the wheel at different times, but generally we choose to stay with the souls we have known lifetime after lifetime. You are certain to see them all again. As for Ronnie and others who may have caused harm, there is no escaping karma."

I suppose that's all anyone can ever ask for, Cade thought. *The opportunity to keep going, to keep learning, and to love again.*

Maybe being dead wouldn't be so bad, especially since it would give him a new chance at life.

A Christmas to Always Remember

CHAPTER ONE

HEAVINESS SETTLED IN HER, BORN of the weight of truth, knowledge, and inertia. If she made her move, indulged in her choice, was she risking too much? But if she did nothing, wasn't she risking the same?

The gray edges of her surroundings came into focus as she listened and waited. The house she occupied had clearly undergone many changes through the years but was still much the same. The hardwood floors were slightly more polished, and the walls had an array of colors customized for each room instead of the previous white, but even with the upgrades and decorating it retained the same sense of place, of belonging, of home.

This was where she belonged, but it got so damn lonely that some days she wondered if she would be consumed by the vacuum that had been created within these walls all those years ago.

That wasn't what mattered now, not the gray edges, not the

new colors, and not what she knew lurked within this world.

This was a new world she was engaged with, a new way of reaching out to others. She would not hesitate any longer. *I want someone who sees me,* she thought. *I want to be heard. But most of all, I want to be known. Truly known.* Pressing the "add friend" button, a mixture of emotions tumbled through her.

Now, all she had to do was wait and watch.

* * *

"Hi, my name is Will, and I'm an alcoholic."

The familiar chorus of "Hi, Will!" sounded before quickly settling into silence. Will hesitated, looking out into the crowd. Even after ten years of standing up and telling his story, apprehension set in before he spoke. Fear of judgment mixed with the desire to reach out to others, to help people in the same way he had been helped. Logically, he knew nobody would laugh at him or make fun of him within those walls. But logic had nothing to do with the butterflies doing gymnastics in his stomach.

"I had my first drink when I was twelve years old," he began. "I thought it would be cool to drink the beer my father had bought for a neighborhood picnic, so I snuck one when I knew nobody was paying attention to me." He stopped for a moment, trying to simply tell the story without holding on to the quagmire of emotions that accompanied it. "I didn't have to worry about getting caught. I wasn't a kid anyone paid much attention to anyway." Images of an average looking young teenager filled his mind. "Nothing was wrong with me, but I didn't stand out. I didn't get in trouble, my grades were okay, and I never had a strong opinion. I never got in the way."

Not that there was anything wrong with staying out of trouble, but in a family with five children, his parents had to focus their priorities on putting out whatever fires his siblings had started first. He didn't blame them for overlooking him, and he knew that it was actually a sign of how much they respected him and thought highly of his maturity at that time that they left him to his own devices. It was just too bad that he wasn't able to live up to their expectations.

"I made sure nobody knew I was drinking, even when I became of legal age," he continued. As he spoke, he held onto the same thought he always had when he told his story. *Please, let me help someone tonight. Let my words reach out to those who need it most.*

Inevitably, after he told his story he felt better. Someone usually came up to talk to him, to share their own story with him, to commiserate on shared misadventures. New people approached him, hoping to absorb his sobriety, hoping that they, too, would be able to stop drinking, maybe even for one night.

Being an alcoholic was deadly for everyone involved.

After the meeting, Will got a cup of coffee at the rickety table leaning in the corner. A small glass bowl with packets of sugar sat next to the powdered milk, the only things that could flavor the not-quite-abysmal coffee. Usually, a tray of store bought cookies sat in the center of the table, and tonight was no exception.

Will stood near the food, Styrofoam cup in hand, glancing around the room. Holding the cup gave him something to do. The chairs for the meeting had already been put away, and people were gathered in groups, talking or lingering on the edge of the room. As usual, Will knew that many wondered if they should say something or leaving quickly, and some were determined not to be one of them.

Suddenly a man stood before him. Will squinted. *Where did he come from?* He didn't remember seeing this guy in the seats, but that didn't mean much. He could have been hovering somewhere else, trying not to be noticed. Will remembered that feeling well, of wanting to fade away and not be seen for who he really was.

Extending his hand, the man said, "Great talk. Very inspiring.

My name is Percy."

"Will," he said, shaking the man's hand. "Thanks. I always say a little prayer that my story will reach someone and help them."

Percy smiled. "I'm fairly confident those prayers are always heard." Will stared at the man in gray who stood before him. Everything about the man was gray, including his hair, his clothing, and… Will squinted again. Yep, even his skin had a grayish tinge to it. *I wonder if he's sick or something. Maybe his liver.*

"I've heard you speak before, but I didn't have time to talk with you," Percy said. "At the meeting over in Gloucester."

"What brings you to Yorktown tonight?"

Percy shrugged, never taking his gaze off of Will. "I felt called to come to this meeting. And I was in town. Hard to ignore that kind of call, right?" When he smiled, Will noticed that the grayness faded from his eyes and a sort of light shined through.

"How long have you been in the program?" Will asked. As he spoke with Percy, the room around them faded at the edges. Will was comforted by this man's presence, and a peace descended over him. He knew without having to be told that Percy had been sober for a while.

"I've been working this program for about thirty years," Percy said. "It's changed how I view the world."

Will nodded. "Yeah, me too. Once I sobered up and started looking around me, I was amazed at some of the things I heard. I am just so grateful to be given a second chance at my life."

"That's rare," Percy said. "So many don't take the chances offered to them, and so many miss the point of life entirely. But your hard work shows, and you are making a difference. That counts for more than you know." Percy reached into his jacket pocket and pulled out a business card. "I'll be in town for a while. Here's my number, if you ever want to talk or get together. I'm trying to connect with some folks in this area."

Will took the card and looked down at the simple lettering. It read:

Percy W.
Consultant
867-5309

"Really?" he laughed. "You have the same phone number as that song?"

Percy grinned. "You would be amazed at the calls I get. It's rather amusing, actually."

"I'll bet. What kind of consulting do you do?"

"You could say I'm a consultant for a higher power. I do a kind of therapy work." Percy glanced behind him. "I won't take up any more of your time. I think there's someone here who wants to speak with you. Feel free to call me whenever you like. And please don't hesitate to call if you need something."

Will peered over Percy's shoulder, but he didn't see anyone approaching. *He probably wants to talk to others.* "Okay. Nice meeting you, I'll give you a call sometime."

Percy's hand enveloped his again, and a warmth flowed up Will's arm, similar to the feeling he would get when his mother wrapped him in a hug. Peace. Love.

Gotta trust my gut instinct, right? He doesn't seem like a crazy person or serial killer. I can't imagine I'd feel so good about someone who hacked up other people with a kitchen knife… then again, maybe that's how they get away with it…

"Excuse me?" The voice to his left was hesitant and soft, almost as if regretting having spoken. "Do you have a moment?"

Will turned and looked into a pair of haunted blue eyes. "Hi, I'm Will."

"My name is Tessa." She shifted from one foot to the other, eyes glancing over the cookie tray and coffee cups. Her body was tensed and a wariness surrounded her. "The thing is, they told me you could help me. And at this point I'm really hoping that's true."

CHAPTER TWO

PERCY HOVERED BEHIND DAHLIA, TRYING to project an authoritative air. "You don't really have the proper permission for this, you know."

As usual, Dahlia ignored him, fiddling instead with the computer. Percy pressed on. "You cannot forget that you are here for a reason, and you have to focus on the reason. Trying something new like that can have unintended consequences."

For a full minute, only the sound of the ticking clock could be heard. Outside, darkness blanketed the landscape. Somewhere in the distance a car door slammed, and a screech owl hooted a warning. The house waited.

Percy didn't have much time to stand there and try to persuade Dahlia of the error of her ways. "You have a job, and you must stick with it. It's what you chose," he whispered.

Dahlia turned to him, her eyes wide. "Yes, I am aware of my choosing. I am aware of every second that the clock ticks off, as

I am aware of the swift passing of time while I do what you refer to as my *job*. But really, what else was I to do? Allow—"

"Dahlia, what is wrong?" Percy interrupted. "Why are you now choosing to step outside of everything you know?"

"Is that why you're here? Because I'm stepping outside of things?" Dahlia's mouth quivered as if she would cry, but no tears came. "I know you might not understand this, but I had to do something. I'm so weary of this existence." She stopped, and Percy said nothing, knowing she needed a moment to pull herself together. Finally, her shoulders gave a small heave, and she continued. "You don't know what it's like, do you? I want someone who sees me. I want to be heard. But most of all, I want to be known, truly known."

Percy was at a loss. He had been sent without instructions, told to find his way the best he could to help Dahlia and the others through the trying events that were to unfold this holiday season. The problem with that was that he was not told exactly what the trying events were going to be, so he was left guessing about an unknown future. "I don't know that this Facebook thing is exactly the way to be seen or heard," he began.

"But I can use it, it's here for me," Dahlia said. "It's easy to use, and I can reach out to others with this tool."

Percy kept quiet. There was nothing he could say, really. He knew every action had a consequence, and Dahlia had started down a path that might have serious consequences. He also knew that when it came to choices, some were not his to make.

Headlights shined on the wall as a car pulled into the driveway. "I cannot stay," Percy said. "But remember, whatever you do, be careful. It's not just you who could get hurt."

* * *

Will pulled into the driveway and checked his rearview mirror one more time. Sure enough, the car was still behind him. After speaking with Tessa, then his sponsor, Rick C., he didn't question anything, he simply let go. Some things in life were meant to be, and he believed that being asked to speak that night was no coincidence.

According to his sponsor, as Will told his story at the meeting, Rick had thought about Will's house. He told Will it was ideal for Tessa since there was an unused apartment built over the detached garage. It had been so long since anyone had lived there that Will never thought about it until he needed the space. He generally didn't lease it out in case one of his family members visited or someone needed a place to stay. Besides, he liked having the privacy and the house all to himself. Not that someone living over the garage would get in the way, but it was another person on his property. This could mean he would occasionally be required to come out of his shell and communicate in some way, and it might even happen before he'd had his morning coffee.

I didn't really need to take that stupid online test to know I'm an introvert. Hell, everyone who knows me knows that.

Tessa had pulled her car into the parking space next to him in the driveway. She sat, apparently waiting for him, probably not wanting to cause trouble. The impression he'd gotten of her was that she wanted to fade away, to be invisible, and not disturb anyone. Her manner suggested a woman not expecting much from anyone and perched to bolt if necessary.

He would not have considered renting his apartment to her if his sponsor hadn't pressed him on the matter. "I can tell you she needs a place to stay, like right now," Rick had said. "Tonight. And I can also tell you she's good for the money. In fact, if she doesn't pay, I'll pay her rent for her. But I can't tell you anything more than that, other than she came to us through other friends in other groups. Can you do this?"

"I'm not worried about the money," Will said. And he wasn't, since he didn't have a big mortgage. He'd bought the house when he'd first gotten sober, and it had been as much of a mess as he was. Because of the disrepair of the house, it was dirt cheap. The first time he'd seen it he'd wanted to cry. The exterior paint was a dirty, faded yellow and peeling from the clapboard, and the center of the home looked as if it were sagging. The inside of the home smelled like grease, mold, and small, dead animals. Parts of the ceiling had collapsed, and Will was careful where he stepped in case the flooring gave way.

"You could only get a rehab loan for this," the Realtor had said with disdain. "I wouldn't go upstairs if I were you, it doesn't look safe. Are you ready to look at the next one?"

"No." Will wasn't ready to look at anything else, because he'd taken one look at the falling down death trap and knew he had to save it. As he stood, quietly assessing what needed to be done, he could swear the house took a deep, raspy breath, as if it were recovering from emphysema. A ray of sunlight slanted through the window, illuminating worn, olive green carpeting. Parts of the kitchen and bathroom had been torn apart, and clearly nothing worked. Built in 1913, the old farmhouse sat on eight acres in Seaford, Virginia. Maybe it was the age of the home, or maybe something in him was responding to the obvious disrepair, but the odd thing was, he felt good here. He felt safe. He felt protected.

Over the years he'd put savings and sweat equity in and remodeled the place so it became an aesthetic haven for him. He wanted a home, not just a pile of wood and wires, and that is exactly what he worked so hard to achieve. Home.

And maybe now he could provide someone else with the same sense of place, a home where she could feel safe. Because Will was pretty sure that at that moment Tessa felt anything but safe. She remained huddled in her car, as if waiting for him to give her a signal that she could exit.

He smiled at her, hoping to be encouraging. Instead, she

shrank back in her seat. *Okay, maybe the smile made me look like a homicidal maniac. Or maybe she wants to stay far away from me.*

Something about Tessa inspired a protective feeling in him, made him want to stand in front of her and defend her with everything he had. Maybe it was the cautious way she held herself, or how she used her long hair to shield her face when she was talking with him. She was pretty, but he also thought she was a bit too thin. *I should have her over for dinner once in a while, try to get her to eat some hearty meals. It looks like she hasn't been eating much for a while.*

Not sure what to do, or how to coax her out of the car, he decided to be direct. "Do you want to see the apartment?" he yelled, as if she were deaf. She nodded and opened her door, but still didn't step out.

"It's empty right now, but it does have furniture," he continued in the same tone of voice.

"Why are you yelling?" she asked.

"I don't know," he said. "You weren't getting out of the car, and I didn't know what to do."

"I wasn't sure what you wanted me to do," she said.

That was an unusual thing to say, but Will was trying not to judge her. Clearly she was working through some emotional debris, but at that moment he was focused on getting her to look at what he hoped would become her new home.

Always trying to save someone or something.

"The stairs are on the side of the garage," he said. "Right this way." And as if she were a stray cat that didn't quite trust humans, she cautiously followed his lead.

One step at a time.

* * *

Tessa wasn't quite sure how to act around Will. She knew he was trying to be nice, but she couldn't stop herself from wondering when he'd change, when he'd start asking for something she didn't want to give. *Are people really this nice? Who the hell is this guy?*

She glanced over at the main house as she climbed the stairs behind him, careful to maintain a good distance so he couldn't reach her if he turned around. She still didn't know who to trust, and she knew that carelessness could cost her her life. But all the self-help books she'd immersed herself in encouraged her to find her inner strength, trust the path before her, and know that all would be well. Easy enough for those who've only dealt with… normal bad times. But no, she couldn't let herself wallow in the past. The future was in front of her, beckoning like a potential friend asking her in for coffee. She could only move forward, and trust that her instincts—and common sense—would guide her.

The front porch to the farmhouse next to the garage was illuminated, and a light was on inside, too. A large elm stood in the front yard, probably providing shade during the height of summer. Crickets sang their chorus, and no traffic could be heard. The house looked warm, inviting… it looked like home. A shudder rippled through her at the thought of home, and she had to force herself to look away. She had to be careful, it might not be good to want too much.

She was grateful for the light illuminating the staircase, and she was also glad that Will simply opened the door and stepped inside. She didn't want to stand too close to him on that little landing at the top of the steps. *Stop it*, she scolded herself. *He's probably just a really nice guy. Not everybody is… bad.*

He had already walked to the other side of the kitchen when she stepped inside.

"As Rick told you, the place is fully furnished and the kitchen is stocked with everything you'll need to cook, but there is no food," Will said. "There are some dry goods, essentials like coffee, but you'll need to make a run to the grocery store. They might still be open if you need something right now."

Her mind was blank as she walked through the space, dazed. The rooms were simple, with neutral colors on the walls and furniture that looked almost new. The scent of cleaner filled the air, as if someone had been expecting her and gotten the place ready.

Tears filled her eyes before she could grab control of her emotions. "Thank you," she said. "I don't know how much you want in rent—"

"One thing at a time," he said. "First, let's sit down and talk. If you want, I can make a pot of coffee."

She shook her head, her stomach sinking at his words. Talk. Whenever someone wanted to talk to her that meant something was coming. Usually it wasn't something good. Although talking was supposed to be a good thing, supposed to clear the air. The books she'd read said that communication was important. *I guess it depends on who you are communicating with.*

She took a breath. She had no choice right now, she had to trust this guy. At least his eyes were kind—without pity when he spoke to her. But once he found out her history, he would probably fall all over himself with the pity thing. Or he'd run away. Or his dark side would come out. Or… Suddenly, she heard the silence in the room. Apparently he had been talking, and now he wasn't. He was waiting for her to comment on whatever he had said.

"Okay," she said. *Keep it vague, he'll never know I wasn't listening.*

"You didn't hear anything I said, did you?" His words were softened by his smile, and the knot in her stomach released.

"Sorry," she said. "I was lost in my thoughts… the space is amazing. The energy here… it feels safe. I don't know how else to describe it."

Will nodded. "That's the exact thought I had the first time I saw the house. It was falling apart, a real mess. But I knew it had good bones. I believe that if you look hard enough, you can find the light shining within anything."

Tessa smiled, her first real smile in a long time. Will hadn't said anything profound, but he'd put her at ease and made her think that maybe, just maybe, everything would be okay.

WILL EASED ONTO THE COUCH with his laptop balanced in one hand and a bowl of popcorn in the other. This was his time to relax, scroll through his email, check Facebook, and watch TV. Simple. Nothing taxing, nothing he had to think about. Tessa was settled safely in the apartment, and he had left her with his phone number in case she needed anything. He flipped through the cable guide, trying to find something good, and settled on a crime show. Opening his laptop, he first checked his email, deleting most of them. Then, he opened his Facebook account. He'd been scrolling for a few minutes, alternating his attention between the television show and reading his friends' updates. After a moment, he noticed he had a friend request.

Dahlia Faith Warren. He frowned, not certain he knew her despite her profile saying she lived in Yorktown. Her profile picture showed a picture of an old-fashioned Singer sewing machine. He clicked over to her timeline, where she actively engaged in conversations with others. *Okay, so she's a real person.* He clicked "Accept Friend Request" and typed in a message on her timeline. "Thanks for the friend request, nice to meet you." He always tried to be polite in his online interactions, especially since noticing that so many lacked social niceties that they might have in a face-to-face conversation.

A blast of heat kicked on as the house shuddered around him. *Damn, I've lost track of time. It's late November already, I'm going to have to get the furnace serviced soon for the winter.*

He was curious about his new friend Dahlia and started clicking through her pictures and information. She had lots of pictures on her profile, but unfortunately none of them were of people. She had plenty of memes and pictures of animals, mostly cats, but he couldn't find any photos of her. *That's kind of strange.* Curious now, he sent her a private message.

Hi Dahlia,

Thanks for reaching out with a friend request. I see that you live in Yorktown. I'm in Seaford. Maybe we've crossed paths before?

Will

Closing his computer, he settled in to watch the rest of the show and finish his popcorn. If he didn't hear back from Dahlia, he would unfriend her. After all, you never really knew who was behind a profile picture.

* * *

Dahlia knew he was there before he said anything, but she wanted to finish typing her answer to Will.

Hi Will,

I don't think we've ever met in person, but I've been in this area for a very long time. Thanks for accepting my request. How do you like living in Seaford? I love this area!

Dahlia

"What in tarnation are you doing?" Percy whispered loudly.

"Shh, you're going to wake Will. He's a light sleeper, you know."

Percy paced behind her, his steps light but clearly agitated. "So, let me get this straight. You have a job to do: protect this house and all who live in it. Yet, here you are, contacting the person who lives here, engaging in some type of conversation, and using his computer to do it… does that cover it?"

"Yes, Percy, I believe that covers it. But you don't understand—"

"What I understand is that you are putting your position in jeopardy as well as possibly causing harm to those you have chosen to protect. This cannot go on."

"But—"

"You know who, and what, we are. We are the ones who stay, the ones who have died but do not cross over. You are spirit, you are not flesh—"

"Others can see us, sometimes. They see you—"

"When we choose to let them see us, yes. But let me remind you: we are the gray ones, the ones whose lives slipped by without purpose, without grabbing hold of what we needed to do to fully appreciate who we could become. You are here to not only grow your own soul but to help others in their journey through this realm."

"That's not fair." Anxiety and despair washed through Dahlia. "I was murdered. I never got the chance to live up to my purpose or grow into who I needed to become. Killed by a darkness so evil that I never stood a chance. And now, I am left here to defend others when it chooses to invade again."

Percy grew quiet for a moment before speaking. "This was your choice. You wanted to stay. Are you choosing otherwise now?"

The night air grew still, and the house itself seemed poised to hear her answer. *Even in this non-physical state, I have fanciful thoughts.* But it was clearly time for her to confess what had been happening.

"Percy, I… I do not understand why I am having these feelings.

Since 1926 I have been here, guarding this house, even during those times it was empty. Always, I have felt that I belonged. But now I am restless, and that makes no sense to me. How can I be restless when I do not have a body? How can I want things that I did not even care for when I was alive?"

She paced around the room, dismayed at the emotions that crashed through her. "What is happening to me?" she whispered.

Percy stepped in front of her and waited to speak until she looked up at him. "I have never seen this before, but you are in a unique situation. Most of the time we are sent to help specific souls through a life event. You, however, have been named sentry of this place, asked to stand guard and wait to dispel evil that might enter. How many times have you been called upon to do so?"

Dahlia didn't have to think about it; each instance of evil entering was seared into her mind. "Many. They came, the dark ones, for whatever reason. I did what I could to banish them. The first time was the hardest. I wasn't sure what to do, but I had to do something."

"What happened that first time?" Percy asked.

Dahlia knew Percy was humoring her, trying to get her to talk, but she answered anyway. Maybe he could help her navigate this distressing situation. "The people who moved into the farmhouse after… after my death, they were distant relatives. Cousins, maybe. I believe they came because they were all the family that was left, so they must have inherited the place. When they first moved in, I was new to this and not entirely certain of my role…" Dahlia stopped as the memories came to her, a series of pictures imprinted from so long ago. "It took me a while to realize what the father was doing to his daughter. Then, when I finally understood what was happening, I pushed him out."

"What do you mean, pushed him out?" Percy said.

"I'm not certain how I did it, but I just sort of—pushed, with my mind, I think. Then one day he decided to leave, and he never came back. It was the best thing for that young girl, really. Once he left them, the mother was so angry with him about his desertion that she probably wouldn't have taken him back if he'd tried."

Dahlia thought about all the times she'd pushed evil away from the house, from the land. All the times she'd followed her purpose. "So many people," she said. "I remember the other killers, not the one who killed me, but the ones who were passing through. Montie Rissell… James Gallagher… Swannie LeMont…"

Percy cocked his head at her. "I know the first name, but I am not familiar with the others. Did they, too, kill?"

Dahlia nodded. "Not here, though, never here. Yes, Montie is still in jail, but the others, they were never caught. I believe the newspapers had names for them, but nobody ever traced them to the killings. But I knew, I could see it around them. So I pushed them away."

"And during that time, did you feel the way you do now?"

"No, that's the strange part." Dahlia started pacing again. "I was very content to know that I was keeping this place safe to be a real home, that I was not allowing the darkness entry to this space. I was doing my job. But little by little I watched people leave, families moving away or people dying, and everything around changing so much. Nobody could see me, I made sure of that. I didn't want the house to get a reputation as haunted; you know how people can talk. Then, for some reason, I wished to be a part of it, to be heard. For heaven's sakes, I once fantasized about Will asking my opinion on what color to paint the walls. What is happening to me?"

"I don't know," Percy said. "But I'll do my best to find out."

* * *

Will held a cup of coffee in one hand and tucked a container of French vanilla creamer in the other. He gently knocked on the door and stepped back, knowing Tessa would be freaked out if he stood too close. When she came to the door, she looked exhausted. Her hair was a tangled mess, as if she'd been running her hand through it, and she had dark circles under her eyes. He tried not to let his surprise show.

"I brought you a cup of coffee to start the morning," he said, holding up the cup. "I don't know what you take in it, but I've got creamer." He stopped talking and waited while she stood before him. Finally, she stepped away from the entry and gestured for him to come in.

"Thank you," she said in a careful tone.

Enough was enough. He couldn't stand seeing her like this. Whatever had happened, she had to know she was safe here. "Listen, I've got to go to work in a little while. I'll leave you my cell phone number in case you need anything. But, seriously, you've got to level with me. Right now you look like crap, like you didn't sleep at all last night. What's going on?"

He knew his approach might be too direct, but he wasn't about to just stand by while someone looked constantly afraid.

She sighed and walked to the kitchen counter, leaning against it as if for support. "I stayed up all night watching the front street. I thought someone was out there."

Will was instantly alert. "Tell me about what you saw."

"A car, parked on the road. Sometime around two a.m. something woke me, and I got up and looked outside. I thought I saw a light on in your house, downstairs, then I noticed a car driving slowly down the street."

I don't leave any lights on at night, Will thought. *Maybe she saw a reflection from a mirror or something.* "Go on," he urged.

"Something about the way the car was driving creeped me out, then it stopped." She closed her eyes for a moment and took a deep breath. "When the car stopped and the headlights went out, I knew it was here to watch this place. It stayed out front until dawn."

Will held up a hand to stop her. "Okay, hold on for just a minute, I need to make a call." He pulled out his cell phone and called the office. "Hey, Mikey, it's Will. Listen, I don't have any interviews lined up this morning, but I wanted to let you know I might be a little bit late coming in. No, everything's fine, I just have to take care of something here. Right. Thanks." Disconnecting, he looked into Tessa's eyes.

"If you believe you were in some kind of danger, it's time for you to tell me what's going on." A look of fear defined her face. "Tessa, listen to me. I don't care what brought you here. I've done things in my life that I don't like people knowing about. I've lied, cheated, stolen, you name it. But if there is a problem then you need to tell me about it. I'm not going to judge you, but I can't help you if I don't know what's going on."

She didn't move, didn't speak. He crossed the room, went to the living room, and sat on the couch. "I'm a reporter, my job is getting information from people. I'm not leaving until you tell me." He knew it was a risk to push her like this, but if she'd been up all night thinking she was in danger then he didn't have the luxury of waiting for her to open up.

Tears began to roll down her cheeks. "I can't," she whispered. "What if I tell you, and…"

"What if you don't tell me and something worse happens?" Will said. "Obviously you're being protected by people in AA, because that's how you got to me. Now all you have to do is tell me what's going on."

After a moment, Tessa straightened and faced him. "What's the worst thing you've ever done?"

Will didn't even have to think about it. "It's kind of a toss-up between a few things. Take your pick of which is the worst." He smiled sadly. "First, I stole my grandmother's engagement ring to buy drugs. I did this the day of my grandfather's funeral, when nobody was in the house." Her eyes widened a bit, and he went on. "Or maybe it was the time I had sex with a person who was not my girlfriend. This was a couple of hours after I had driven drunk and wrecked the car, sending my girlfriend to the hospital." She looked even more surprised, which was good. Maybe this would help her open up. "And if you were listening to my story the other night, you'd know the part about stealing my parents' credit card numbers so I could do whatever it was I thought I was going to do." He waved his hand in the air. "So, take your pick of what was the worst thing, I've done them all. And I thank God that I'm sober now, that I don't do that same kind of stupid crap that hurt so many people just so I could get my stupid fix. I'm grateful that's all over. Your turn."

She hung her head and spoke so softly he had to strain to hear her. "I sold myself."

"For drugs?"

When she shook her head no, he was confused. "You're talking about sex, right?"

She nodded. "I did it because I had to."

He waited a moment, and when she didn't add anything, he stopped himself from questioning her. Her hands were shaking, and a nasty suspicion was taking root in his mind.

"I was sixteen years old when I was first approached by someone I thought was a friend," she said. "At least, I wanted him to be a friend. He was really cute, and I was not a popular kid. But he was interested in me, and he was always there."

"How old was this guy?" Will asked.

She shrugged. "He said he was eighteen. I don't know if it was true or not, because I found out later that he was a scout."

Will was confused. "A boy scout?"

A faint smile crossed Tessa's face, the first he'd seen all morning. "No, he was a scout for another person. His job was to find kids like me and lure me to his boss."

Will had never heard of this before. "What do you mean, kids like you?"

Tessa's faint smile was replaced by a grimace, as if she were in pain. "I was an awkward kid, shy and not really pretty at all. Plus, I was in the foster care system, and at that time I was on my tenth or eleventh placement, I can't remember. Maybe it was number twelve, who knows."

Will was stunned. "Wait a minute, do you mean that you lived in more than ten foster homes?"

Tessa nodded. "Yes. I guess I was difficult to place but I'm not sure why. I'd be living somewhere then the next thing I knew the social worker would show up and tell me it was time to go."

He was having trouble imagining what this would be like for her as a young kid. Definitely not a traditional childhood, that's for sure. "Was this here, in Virginia?"

She shook her head. "No, in Florida. They weren't very good at checking up on me, and I only saw the worker when it was time to move. So when this boy, who said his name was Joey, asked me to run away with him, it seemed like a good idea at the time. It's not like I had any family who cared, anyway. I left a note for the family and hopped in the car with Joey."

"But it wasn't what you thought," Will said.

"Not even a little bit." Tessa stopped talking again and began to pace. Then she stopped, and as if making up her mind, looked Will directly in the eye. "Joey took me to the guy he worked for, who for the past decade has kept me as his worker. I was fed and given a place to stay, but I had to have sex with the men he arranged. At first, I wouldn't do it, but…" Her voice trailed off as her face took on a faraway look. "This guy, he knew what he was doing…"

Will almost hated to know, but if he was going to help her in any way, he had to get the information. "What could be worse than being forced to have sex with strangers?"

Tessa shook her head, as if wondering how Will had become so naïve. *I'm kind of wondering the same thing. How did I not know about this? How the hell did this girl survive any of that?*

"In the beginning, he must have known how I'd act. I wasn't the only girl, and he'd built quite the business. So, he bought me a puppy. A golden retriever, a sweet little baby. And whenever I'd refuse to do what he told me to do, he wouldn't say anything, but he would hurt the puppy." She paused and took another breath, as if trying to control her emotions. "I tried not to care, but I couldn't stand that I was the reason for all the yelping and crying. He hurt my dog, so I felt like I had no choice. I know how stupid that sounds—"

"Actually, it sounds brave," Will said. "Anybody who would sacrifice themselves to help an innocent animal is more than a decent human being. You're a hero."

Tessa actually laughed then. "I think you're being a little dramatic."

"Compared to what I've done in my life? No, I don't think so. I'm assuming you ended up in AA after you got away from this guy?" He knew he was taking a chance asking, but he'd come this far in her story, so he might as well hear the whole thing.

"Yes. Brian—that's the guy who was in charge of me—would give me something to drink, usually vodka, before he'd send me out. Said it would loosen me up, make me more fun. Pretty soon I needed it just to get through my days. I tried to tell him I didn't want any, but he didn't care about that. He poured it down my throat. Literally. So once I… got away, I tried not to drink. But I needed help, so I started going to meetings."

Will stood, walked back to the kitchen, and peered through the blinds at the street outside. He knew that the next part of the conversation was the important part, so he didn't want to rush her. Hopefully his face betrayed nothing, but anger roiled his stomach. People who trapped others into those types of situations were evil, pure and simple. Although he'd had many conversations with friends about truth, goodness, and evil in this world, there was no question about this. Darkness had invaded Tessa's life, and he knew he would do whatever he needed to do to keep it at bay. Permanently.

He waited a minute, then asked, "How did you get away?"

"Luck," Tessa said. "And books." Will raised his eyebrows, not sure he'd heard her correctly. She stood straighter, as if thinking about books gave her courage. "He had this one customer I had to meet at the library. A regular. Sometimes I had to wait for him, and sometimes he wouldn't show up. There wasn't much I could do; Brian was always watching me, so I told him that I needed to look like I was there for a reason. I would take books off of shelves and start reading. I tried reading lots of different kinds of books: mysteries, teen, nonfiction, but the ones I liked the best were the self-help books."

Will's respect for Tessa grew. Here was a woman who had endured pain of all kinds, who was truly able to help herself and get out of a terrible situation.

"After a while, I realized all the books had the same theme," she continued. "I had the power to free myself, the ability to make my life what I wanted it to be. One day, I did the unthinkable. I tore a page out of a book, angled myself so nobody could see what I was doing and wrote a note in the book. Then I approached the librarian. Brian was watching, but I was very careful. All he heard me say was that I was reporting a vandalized book. Two days later the detectives were there, waiting for me. It all happened so quietly, I was amazed. All this time I'd been living with this monster, then one day it just ended."

But Will knew better. He knew what it meant that someone was watching the place all night. "It hasn't ended, though, has it?"

She shook her head, tears threatening to spill yet again. "No, it hasn't."

CHAPTER FOUR

THE LATE AFTERNOON SUN WARMED the front room of the farmhouse, dancing off of the gleaming mahogany sideboard and settling in as the clock ticked comfortably. Dahlia wandered through the rooms, once again enjoying what Will had done to the house. *He has a wonderful eye*, she thought. *He's made it into a real home, brought a sense of peace to this place.*

Still, something was bothering her. A feeling of disquiet shivered through her, the sense that the energy around her was off. *It's almost as if I'm waiting for something bad to happen. I hope not…* She thought about the new tenant over the garage, Tessa. Dahlia had seen her the few times she'd been over, and she wondered what was simmering between Tessa and Will. Tension often lined Tessa's face, and Will acted as her protector, even in his own home. She knew Tessa had faced something terrible and survived, and she admired the woman greatly for this. *Perhaps this has something to do with what she's been through.*

Dahlia wandered into the front hallway and stood before the mirror that hung over the antique regency console table. She stared for a moment, then decided to do it. *Why not? If I want to be seen, then I have to be able to let people see me.*

Dahlia hadn't spent much time trying to appear to people, since her primary focus at the house was keeping evil at bay. It had never occurred to her that she should appear, ever. But things were changing, and as she had said to Percy she wasn't sure why she was having these feelings. All she knew was that she felt more compelled than ever to try to appear.

Right now, she thought. *It's as good a time as any.*

Focusing, she closed her eyes. She wasn't exactly certain how this worked, but she began with the idea that she could be seen. *I am present, I am visible…*

She slowly opened her eyes and smiled. Her reflection in the mirror smiled back at her. Maybe this wouldn't be too difficult after all.

"What the hell are you doing in my house?" The voice made her jump.

"Will?" she said.

"How do you know my name? And answer my question: what the hell are you doing here?"

She wasn't sure how to answer. This had never happened to her before, and she didn't know what to do. She might be dead, but that didn't stop the nauseous feeling that swept through her.

"Listen, it's not what you think," she began. "I have a reason for being here—"

"Start with your name. I want to know your name, right now." His face was thunderous, and he loomed over her. If she didn't know better she might have thought he would hurt her, but this was Will. He wouldn't hurt anybody, not intentionally.

But he could see her. He could absolutely see her. Only this probably wasn't the best time for that to happen, as much as she'd wanted it. She had no choice but to answer him.

"I'm Dahlia," she whispered. "Dahlia Faith Warren." His silence was like a storm, with dark emotions reaching out and swirling all around the room. *Does he even remember how he knows me?*

"What?" he exploded. "The girl from Facebook?"

When she nodded, his face got red. "I don't know what your story is, or what kind of game you're playing, but this is as far as it goes. We're done here. You need to leave, now."

She felt the energy start to siphon out of her. "You-you're telling me to go? From this house?"

"Right now. And don't come back."

"But you don't understand—" It was too late. He'd already turned his back on her, and didn't see her fade away to nothingness after banishing her from the place she had sworn to protect.

* * *

Percy stepped into the valley, uncertain about what had happened. Large rock formations rose up around him, dark figures that were almost menacing. The light was gray, creating a grim color palette in the barren landscape. Dahlia sat in the center of the valley with her arms wrapped around her bent legs and her head resting on her knees. She must have heard him approach because she spoke without looking at him. "I have failed."

He waited a moment before answering. This was going to be tricky, he knew, and his answer must somehow sustain her for what might possibly come. "There are always many different outcomes to any situation. We don't yet know what will happen."

She looked at him then, empty and void of emotion. Percy didn't know what to make of this being in front of him. He'd never known Dahlia to be so… hollow, even after she'd been murdered.

"Do you remember?" she asked. "A long time ago, but not

really. 1926."

Confusion laced his thoughts as he tried to figure out what she meant. "Remember?"

Then, as if she had sent him a vision, he could see it. The scene before him played out with an excruciating inevitability; something he was powerless to not see.

The blinding blue sky wrapped the lilac-scented world. A soft, early summer wind blew, and at first only silence reigned. Then, the noises began to intrude. The buzzing of cicadas. Birdsong punctuating the breeze. Crisp shadows indicating the late afternoon. And the gentle humming from a woman hanging laundry on the clothesline behind the farmhouse.

The woman outside was the only person evident at the cheery yellow farmhouse. In the distance, a low rumbling came from a cloud of dust. She looked up and smiled at the sight. By the time the car had parked in the front driveway, she had put down her clothes and rushed out to greet him.

But her smile faded as he strode toward her. Panic replaced delight, and she turned to run, a fruitless endeavor. He caught her easily, grabbed her long hair, and pulled her head back. He then shoved a knife into her abdomen and dragged her around the house to the entry of the basement.

The vision cleared. Percy was once again alone with Dahlia in a dark, barren world. "His name was Charles. He was my husband, you know. He got away somehow. But once I realized I was dead, that my life had been stolen from me, I made the decision that I would never again allow that kind of evil to creep back. I would stand with the light and not allow the darkness in. I made a promise, one that I can no longer keep."

She looked at Percy then, still blank. "What is to happen to me now?"

"I don't know," he said. "But I'm going to do everything I can to help you."

"And Will," she added. "Because I think he's going to need it. I don't know how I know this, but the darkness is returning. And this one feels the same."

"What do you mean?"

Dahlia did not hesitate to answer. "This one feels just like the other evil. The one that killed me the first time."

CHAPTER FIVE

TESSA PUT HER HAND ON Will's arm in an effort to comfort him. He appreciated her concern, but at that moment her touch was somewhat distracting. He did nothing to remove her hand, as he knew that even that slight show of caring was an effort for her. She'd come a long way in recovering from being a sex trafficking victim, but some things were still difficult, like getting close to people.

"How did she get in?" Tessa asked.

Will shook his head. Never mind how she got in, how did she leave? He had turned his back on his unwanted guest, and she simply vanished, as if she had never been there.

"This whole thing is just really strange," he said. "I don't know, it feels off somehow. I can't really explain why, it just…"

"Having someone come into your house is going to leave you feeling violated," Tessa said. "It's kind of a weird thing to do."

Will agreed. "But there's more to it than that." He hesitated, wondering how much to tell her. "I'm going to tell you something, but you have to promise me that you won't get weirded out or think I'm insane or need to see a psychiatrist." Tessa stiffened beside him, so he hurried to add, "It's about Dahlia."

She looked at him, concern evident in her eyes. "I promise to *try* not to think you're crazy."

"Try?"

She laughed and shook her head. "C'mon, that's the best you're going to get without me knowing what you're going to say."

"Then I guess I'll have to take it." He took a deep breath before continuing. "The thing is, I keep feeling like I've made a mistake."

"You think kicking out a complete stranger who broke into your house is a mistake?"

"No, that's not what I meant. I don't think she's a complete stranger." *This is where it's going to get weird*, he thought. *But I've got to say it to someone.* "Listen, Tessa, I trust you. And I know how this is going to sound, so I'm going to take a chance and say it. To you. But probably nobody else, okay?" After Tessa nodded, he continued. "When I walked in and saw Dahlia standing there, I knew who she was."

"Because she lives in the area," Tessa said. "You've seen her around here before?"

Will shook his head. "No, I've never seen her outside of this house. But... I've seen her before. Here."

"I don't understand," Tessa said. "She's broken in before? When?"

"I'm not sure she broke in, exactly. The thing is, I've caught glimpses of her in weird places, but I thought I was dreaming or seeing things. And each time I've seen her it's been as if she was not quite clear, like I was seeing her in a fog or something, and it's always been really fast then she disappeared. Or I would catch a glimpse of her in a mirror, then she was gone. But not like a real person was here, more like a... Crap. How should I say this?"

"A ghost?" Tessa offered.

Will tried not to look at her, knowing he might see judgement or pity or both. Instead, he focused on trying to push his inexplicable sadness away. "I suppose you could say that."

The house no longer felt like a home. Instead, it felt empty, and the warm feeling he'd gotten when he'd first seen the place was no longer there. Not only that, it didn't feel safe, but he didn't know if that was because he was worried that someone was watching Tessa or if... *Or if you're crazy*, he thought.

"Listen." Tessa moved to sit in front of Will so he could see her face. "I don't think you're crazy. I think you've probably seen someone, or something, here, and maybe this person looked like the woman who came in. Maybe she's a relative or something. But here's the thing: you're not going to be happy until you figure this out. So why don't you try to contact her, talk to her, and see what she wanted? Obviously you didn't get a chance to talk when you saw her, so maybe you can find her and ask some questions."

A flash of hope pierced his inertia. "You're right, that's exactly what I should do. Thank you."

She stood, pulling him up with her. "It's always easier to help other people figure out what to do instead of yourself. C'mon, let's get to the AA meeting. I think being with your sponsor and friends will make you feel better, too."

He held her hand as they left, in a friendly gesture more than anything else. But it felt right to do that, it felt right to be next to her and talking about life, leaving to go somewhere together. "It's Christmas eve tomorrow," he said. "When was the last time you celebrated the holidays?"

He thought he knew the answer, but once again, Tessa surprised him. "I celebrated it every year. I would find a way to give thanks, to say a prayer to the Great Spirit or the little baby Jesus, who I imagined as looking very different than the pictures they try to shove at us, and I would try to sneak a piece of greenery into a fire or breathe in goodness or just offer up general thanks for being alive."

"Really?" He tried to imagine what it would have been like for her, but he couldn't. He simply could not picture the scene she had just painted, and it angered him that she had been forced to endure the pain of that type of slavery.

"I remember reading in one of those books how important gratitude is, no matter what. I'd made up my mind that my life would not continue to be what it was. I didn't know how, and I didn't know when, but I knew I'd get out sooner or later. Besides, having an internal Christmas celebration was the best way to say F-you to the man who tried to control me."

As they walked out the door and he locked it behind him, Will marveled at Tessa's ability to adapt to a life not at all of her choosing. Plus, she was insightful and kind, a combination that intrigued and attracted him. *Slow down, boy, she's just come off a really bad experience. You can't mess things up for her.*

At the very least he could protect her. Because as he pulled out of the driveway with her in the passenger seat, he saw the SUV parked down the street. And he knew, without having to be told, that whoever was in it was waiting for her.

Let them come, he thought. *Let them try to get through me and my friends and hurt her.*

He was ready.

* * *

The weather had grown colder, and a damp chill permeated the air. Christmas decorations punctuated the area; wreaths on doors, light-up reindeer on lawns, and Christmas trees outlined in picture windows. Percy stood outside the church, waiting for Will. He greeted everyone who walked past him to go to the AA meeting, smiling and sending positive thoughts at those who were there to heal. *What is this situation going to do to Will's sobriety?* This was the first time that thought had occurred to Percy, but he pushed the question away. Percy knew that everything unfolded in its own time, and he simply had to trust the process and believe that all would work out for the best. Besides, Will had been in constant contact with his sponsor and a multitude of others from the program lately. *He's been so busy talking with the others that he really hasn't even had a moment to spare,* Percy thought. *He's not answering his phone, either. And it's not like I can just show up at his house. This is too important.*

Percy knew he had to find a way to talk face-to-face with Will tonight. He couldn't take the chance that Will would be distracted or not hear him. Plus, mixed in with all the canned holiday music wafting through the air right now was something else… an odor or an image or a darkness that Percy could not quite catch, an energy that hovered just beyond the edge of normalcy and siphoned off of others. He could feel it, whatever it was, and he knew it was not ready to go away. He knew it was ready to create more complications.

Will and Tessa got out of the car that had just parked. Percy watched them, noting that their bond had strengthened in the short time they'd known each other. He smiled. Love during the Christmas season was very special.

He raised his arm and waved as Will approached the steps. "Will, my friend, it's been a while. How are you?"

Will smiled and hugged Percy. "Great to see you. Should be a good meeting, tonight, right?"

Percy nodded and spoke before Will could walk away. "I hate to impose, because I know how busy you are, but I need to talk with you, Will. It's very important." When Will hesitated and looked at Tessa, Percy rushed to finish what he needed to say. "I don't mind at all if Tessa is there; in fact, it would probably be better if she was. Truly, I wouldn't disturb you if I didn't feel this was critical."

"Does this have anything to do with Tessa?" Will asked, taking a combative posture.

Percy made a soothing gesture with his hands. "No, not directly. But it does impact you, so I think that would affect her." He looked at both of them standing in front of him. "I have the impression that if something serious is going on with one of you then the other would want to know, right?"

Will nodded. "Okay, let's talk after the meeting. Can you at least tell me what this is about? It's not really fair to leave me hanging, you know."

Percy hesitated before speaking, but he knew he had to be honest. "It's about Dahlia. I have some information I'd like to share with you."

Will's gaze was piercing. Finally, he let out a big sigh. "In that case why don't we go back to my house tonight. I have a feeling this could take a while."

CHAPTER SIX

WILL TOOK HIS TIME LIGHTING the fire in the fireplace. The house was cold lately, and despite turning the thermostat up a couple of degrees the chill in the air would not dispel. He couldn't help but wonder if the lack of warmth had something to do with Dahlia. *That's crazy. But I can't stop thinking there's a connection that I've missed.*

"Have you noticed that the house has been cold lately?" Tessa said, echoing Will's thoughts. "The apartment is like that, too. It feels like an Arctic blast has pushed its way in and taken root in these buildings."

"I think it's from the recent events that have happened here," Percy said from the couch. He and Tessa were seated, watching Will as he stepped back from the roaring blaze he'd just constructed. When Will sat in the wingback chair facing them, he said, "Let's talk. How do you know Dahlia?"

Percy sat very still for a moment. Will knew he was struggling with his thoughts, and he allowed Percy a moment to speak. "I have a newspaper article I'd like to show you." Reaching into a computer bag that he had carried in with him, Percy pulled out a stack of yellowed papers. "You need to be careful reading these, the newspaper is quite old and brittle."

Will leaned forward and looked at the banner on the newspaper. "The Richmond Dispatch… wait… 1926?"

When Percy nodded, Will reached out, picked up the paper, and scanned the front page. "Am I supposed to be reading the headline article?"

"No, the article below the fold. On the bottom of the first page."

Will flipped the paper over. The picture stared back at him, sending a jolt of electricity through his body. When Tessa came and stood next to him, he angled the paper so she could get a better look at it. "That's her, isn't it?" Tessa asked.

"It must be someone related to her," Will said. "Because it looks exactly like her."

"No, I'm sorry, but Tessa is correct. The picture on the front page is Dahlia," Percy said.

"It can't be. This paper is from 1926. Is the paper real?" Will said, turning it over and examining it to determine authenticity.

"The paper is real," Percy said. "And I'm sorry if I upset you, but I think it's time you knew the truth."

"She lived here, didn't she?" Tessa said. "It makes sense, what Will was saying about how he would see her sometimes but she wasn't really there. She died here, didn't she?"

* * *

Tessa didn't know why the men were so surprised when she said that. The article in front of her was very clear: *Woman Murdered At Farmhouse.* Seriously, she'd have to be an idiot not to connect the dots on this.

But sometimes it took people a bit longer to believe what was right in front of them. Maybe her life experience opened her up to different concepts about reality, but she had no trouble whatsoever with the idea that things existed outside of the "normal" that most people lived with. Quickly scanning the article, the coldness that had seeped through her body seemed to intensify. Almost shivering, she looked up at Will.

"She didn't just die, she was murdered," Tessa said. "Here. At this house." Pointing at the article, Tessa continued to read. "It says that because they found so much blood in the front yard, plus the drag marks, they believe whoever did it killed her and stuffed her in the basement." Tessa looked up, tears swimming in her eyes. "They never found the husband, did they?"

Percy shook his head. "You are correct, they never found the husband. But—"

"Will, you've got to get her back," Tessa said. "Now."

Will's face was a blend of confusion and fear. "I don't know what you—"

"How did she leave?" Tessa asked, a note of impatience in her voice. "When you kicked Dahlia out of the house, which door did she walk out of?"

Will slumped against the back of the chair and let out a breath. "I don't know. I asked her to leave, then she was gone. I never actually saw her go out a door or anything. She was here, then she wasn't."

"Exactly," Tessa said. "She faded into wherever she went, but she's not here with us. I think you banished her."

"What are you talking about?" Will said, practically yelling. "This whole thing doesn't make any sense. She was some crazy chick who got on Facebook and pretended to be someone, then she showed up here—"

A sense of urgency gripped Tessa. If she had learned one thing in her life, one life-saving thing, this was it: always trust your instincts. And right now her instincts were screaming at her that they had to find a way to get Dahlia back, in this house, before it was too late.

CHAPTER SEVEN

TESSA'S FEAR ALMOST PARALYZED HER. Something very dark was coming, she could feel it. "Hurry, Will, call her back, before it's too late."

"What are you talking about?" Will said. "Before what's too late? You're safe here, calm down. Maybe you're right, but I can't just get on Facebook—"

"No, you don't do it on Facebook. You have to invite her in, or something like that. Or ask her to be here, I don't know," Tessa said. "Percy, how does this work?"

Percy nodded. "She's right. Dahlia is—was—the guardian spirit of this house. Her job was to protect the residents from any evil that might try to get in. When you told her she had to go, she had no choice but to leave. I do not believe she can come back unless you invite her in."

"You don't believe? Don't you know for sure?" Will asked.

Percy shook his head. "No. I've never dealt with this type of situation before."

"Who are you?" Will said. "You're not who you said you are."

"I am exactly who I said I am. Remember I told you I worked for a higher power?"

"You said you were a therapist."

Percy shrugged. "That's part of it. But I do a sort of consulting work here, and I try to help those I've been assigned to help. This particular assignment is somewhat different from anything I've ever done before."

The ticking of the clock blended with the sound of Tessa's labored breathing. They didn't have time for this conversation, action needed to happen now. A wave of dark dread descended on the house. *How can they not feel that? How can they stand there as if nothing were happening?*

"You need to do something," Tessa whispered, immobilized by her own emotions.

"I think we need to sit down and talk about this some more," Will said.

Tessa turned and walked to the front window, where the starless night lay stretched wide like a trap. Will kept talking. "I'm not saying I don't believe you, but we need to approach this in a rational way. Let's start with what we know, and then we can formulate a plan."

A humming started inside Tessa, as if her insides were made from taut violin strings. Her mouth was dry and her hands shook. *Can they hear it?* she wondered. *Do they know it's coming from me, that screeching sound?*

She knew without turning around that Will had sat in the chair again, but Percy remained standing. "Tessa, it's going to be okay," Will said.

"No, it's not," she answered. "You need to call her back right now. Stop waiting to talk, stop wondering what's going on, just call her. Now."

"Why?" Will said.

"Because he's here," she answered as a wave of headlights washed through the room.

* * *

Dahlia couldn't remember being born, but she decided it must have been very much like what was happening right now. Opening before her, a large whirlpool pulled her in with a gentle whooshing sound, and she hurtled her way through the tunnel-like structure toward the end. The sensation was not unpleasant, but she definitely had no control or ability to move. Gentle waves of energy pulsed over her and propelled her into the house she had come to love and consider home. The main difference was that this time nobody could see her.

Both Will and Percy stood as if frozen. Will had his hands in front of him in a placating gesture, clearly trying to calm whoever was in the house. "I don't think this is a very good idea. The police are on the way. And so is Dahlia."

Tessa was moving away from the window, inching toward the kitchen. Dahlia knew she was trying to be unobtrusive, but unfortunately the intruder was fixated on her.

The intruder laughed, an ugly sound that Dahlia knew well. "Nobody is on the way, kid. And don't worry, I'll make it painless for you and the old man."

"Leave them alone," Tessa said in a hoarse voice. "They didn't do anything. Will, where is she?"

The snarl was evident in the man's voice. "Nobody's coming to save you, sugar. And these guys have been harboring stolen property. I think that constitutes a crime."

"She's not property," Will yelled, lunging at the man. His punch was easily blocked by the man, who then raised a large metal pipe over his head and slammed it onto Will. Will crumpled into a heap on the ground. He then turned and slammed the same pipe into Percy's center. The pipe made a thudding sound when it connected, and Percy collapsed without a whimper.

"Easier than shooting, don't you think, sugar?"

Tessa stood next to the hutch that held an array of fine china and crystal. Dahlia pushed aside the fear that threatened to consume her. *So, he's back. This is what I've been waiting for.*

"Why aren't you in jail?" Tessa said.

"Because you are mine," the man said. "Because lawyers and judges and anybody in the world can be bought, and after that I get to come back and finish my business. Let's go." He made an impatient gesture. "If you won't come with me, I'll just kill you. I don't want to leave any loose ends, but I think I've spent enough time on you."

Dahlia drifted over to where Tessa stood, touching her lightly on the shoulder so that the woman would know she was not alone. *She is very sensitive, and I'm sure she felt that.* When Tessa straightened a little taller, Dahlia knew she was right. Tessa had felt her presence.

Dahlia continued to push on Tessa, edging her back toward the window. *Because I've waited all these years for this, to defend others from this exact evil.*

The man turned slightly, mocking Tessa. "What the hell do you think you're doing, getting ready to jump out the window?"

Almost… almost…

"She's only doing what I asked," Dahlia said, forcing herself to appear. A multitude of emotions crossed the man's face: confusion, fear, and finally, anger.

"Hello, Charles," Dahlia said as she drifted up toward the ceiling. "I can't say it's good to see you again, but this time I'm not going to let you get away with killing another innocent woman."

"What the hell—" Charles advanced toward Dahlia, fury in his movements. "What kind of trick is this? Do I know you—wait, yes, I—"

"You bet," Dahlia said as she shoved the hutch with all her might. Tessa hopped a little more out of the way as the heavy oak piece of furniture crashed down upon Charles. The noise of the falling piece and breaking glass resounded through the room. Dahlia grinned at Tessa. "And that, my dear, is how we take care of bad guys. Are you okay?"

CHAPTER EIGHT

SNOW FELL GENTLY THROUGH THE night, obscuring any ugliness that marred the landscape. Percy knocked on the door and waited, hoping that Tessa and Will liked carrot cake. It was all he could find on such short notice.

Tessa laughed when she opened the door and saw what Percy was holding. "Come in, please," she said. "It's kind of cold out there."

"That usually happens around this time of year. Merry Christmas!"

"Is that Percy?" Will hollered from the kitchen.

"Yes," Tessa laughed. "And he made us a carrot cake to go with our dinner."

"I wish I could taste it."

"Dahlia!" Percy said. "It's so wonderful to see you again."

"You mean now that I'm not pushing large pieces of furniture onto bad people?" Dahlia smiled as she said this, but Percy knew she held a hint of remorse at having to hurt another. Even if it was the man who had hurt her so long ago.

"Are you feeling okay?" he asked.

Dahlia glanced at Will, who had emerged from the kitchen, and Tessa, who was smiling at her. "I am wonderful. I am here in this beautiful home, with these amazing people. I have finally faced the man who killed me—"

"This still doesn't make any sense to me," Will said. "How could that guy be the one who killed you in 1926?"

"Reincarnation," Tessa said, nudging him with her elbow. "I've explained all this to you."

"But it still doesn't explain how she knew it was the same guy. It's not like they looked the same or anything," Will said.

"I recognized his true self," Dahlia said. "His spirit was right there for me to see it."

Percy crossed the room and handed the cake to Will. "I'm just glad everything worked out. And I assume that now that you are aware of Dahlia you will allow her to remain?"

Will nodded. "Of course. Since everything happened… my life, it's not the same. I don't think it ever will be. But Dahlia has spent so much time taking care of…" Percy waited, knowing that Will was overwhelmed with emotion. "She can stay, but she knows the rules." He leveled a look at her.

Dahlia put one hand on her hip and held up a finger. "First, no going in Will's room." She held up a second finger. "And no going in the bathroom." Then she held up a third finger. "And no scaring the guests. Easy peasy, I can do this."

Percy smiled, marveling again at how things had worked out. "And Tessa, how is your apartment?"

"Much better," Tessa said. "Especially now that Dahlia comes to visit. We like to play card games and talk."

Percy raised his eyebrows. "Card games?"

Will called over his shoulder as he walked back into the kitchen.

"It's not the card games I'm worried about, it's the talking."

Percy smiled. The dining room table had already been set, and the dishes and glasses sparkled. "I thought you broke everything…"

"We did," Tessa said. "But Will had an entire attic full of stuff that had belonged to his grandmother. It was kind of fun going through it all and pulling out things we could use for our Christmas dinner. Are you hungry?"

Percy didn't tell her that no, he wasn't hungry. Because of what he was, he never got hungry. But he could sit and eat with them, sharing a meal and the warmth of Christmas. They probably had more questions, and he was ready to provide answers. They were good people who had faced darkness and won. Because of that, he was fairly certain this was one Christmas they would always remember.

A Different
Kind of Christmas

CHAPTER ONE

HOPE STOOD AND STRETCHED, HER hands dirty from the soil. Despite the chill in the air, the afternoon sun was bright, causing her to squint in despair at the fragile patch of garden. Hopefully she had done it right this time. She had spent all morning weeding and spraying soapy water on her plants, nurturing them with water saved in barrels from the rains. She was hoping and praying that something edible grew even this late in the year, but she'd never had to try to grow food in the winter before. Her late summer garden had been a dismal failure. What did she know about farming or food? For that matter, what did she know about starting her whole world over?

Absently wiping sweat from her forehead, she tried not to panic about her dwindling supply of rations. Most people couldn't use the grocery stores anymore, never mind any of the other luxuries from what she thought of as "back then." *Never mind*, she decided. *No sense wasting time longing for the past when the present has so many troubles.*

"Mommy, do you need any help?" Sandy, her six-year-old daughter, walked into the backyard holding a bucket. Hope smiled, trying to hide her weariness. Her ten-year-old son Jared, silent as a shadow, stood behind his sister.

"Thanks, guys, but I think I'm okay for now. Everything's taken care of. You can play for a little while, but later this afternoon I'll need help starting the fire for supper." Watching them start to wander toward the front yard, she held her tongue. They were good kids, and they knew the rules. Besides, this was probably one of the last warm days they'd have for a while. November in this part of Virginia was odd, it could be warm one day and freezing the next. But for her the weather wasn't the problem, letting go of the constant fear that something else was going to happen was the difficult part.

Sandy turned and looked at her. "I'll be up in the tree," Sandy said solemnly.

Hope sighed. She wasn't sure what to do about this behavior, or if she should do anything at all. "Okay, honey, you go ahead. Just be careful climbing into the lookout."

Jared's gaze was piercing as he stared at his mother. She felt the heat of anger coming off him. Just as she didn't know what to do with Sandy, she had no idea how to handle Jared. Some days she thought about giving up, but that wasn't a real option. She refused to be defeated by the circumstances.

"You shouldn't let her do that, you know," he spoke defiantly. "Dad's not coming back, and you shouldn't let her think he is."

"We don't know that for certain, honey. We don't even know what happened to him, so there's always hope." Hope spoke quietly, trying to offer some measure of reassurance to a son that had to grow up so quickly.

"C'mon, Mom, he left to go find food and whatever, but we know what's out there. He probably got beaten and left to die somewhere. You've gotta stop kidding yourself."

Birdsong erupted behind her, and for just a moment Hope closed her eyes, almost able to lull herself into believing everything was as it had been before. She could almost do it, too. The sun was warm against her face, and the stillness of the neighborhood was typical of any suburban area. The middle class homes stood solid and reassuring, homes where families ate together and laughed together. Homes where phones rang constantly, relatives visited and neighbors dropped by to say hello. They lived in a neighborhood with nice houses and no crime, a great place to raise the kids. The grass was always mowed, flower gardens were lovingly tended, and people always waved in greeting.

Until it all collapsed. When the financial crisis loomed, everyone shrugged it off. "This has happened before, we'll get through it," was the collective thought. Everyone watched as Europe teetered and fell over the precipice of disaster, and tried to ignore what was happening. After all, a great big ocean separated Europe from the United States. But instead of recovery, an international economic collapse occurred this past spring. Banks closed, real estate lost all value, and stock markets around the world were a joke.

Hope supposed it had been inevitable and they had all missed the warning signs, but she, like most everyone else, was taken completely by surprise. Once the United States fell, despair loomed worldwide. The people of the United States, used to modern comforts, struggled to survive this new catastrophe.

Hope could never have predicted a situation like this. On television, sure, because that wasn't real. But in Yorktown, Virginia, it hardly seemed possible.

Spring stretched into summer and then fall and now winter; nothing got better. They no longer had fuel to drive the cars. The electricity had gone out in August. Computers sat gathering dust while refrigerators were used as storage for whatever could be picked, gathered, or grown. Squirrels and rabbits, once constant garden nuisances, were now in short supply. And husbands went off to try to find food and information and never came home. Hope sighed in frustration, feeling a pain in her chest.

If only I hadn't let him leave by himself, if only we knew back then that nobody should go out alone…

She forced her thoughts away from the past and tried to focus on what she needed in the moment. *Maybe we can gather the leaves and use them in fires. We've got enough leaves in the yard now.*

Jared continued to stare at her as her thoughts raced. "I know you think your sister is wasting her time, but right now she needs to be up there looking for Dad. It makes her feel better to think she's on lookout for him. This is just as hard for her as it is for you, sweetie."

"Mom! Jared!" Jared and Hope jumped, startled by the tone in Sandy's voice. "Mr. Conway is here."

As she hurried to the front yard, Hope felt a moment of unrest. She always had that feeling when Marty Conway stopped at their house. An ex-army officer, Marty had taken on patrol responsibility and security for the neighborhood. During the day he could be seen riding his bike, armed and in uniform, watching for any sign of trouble from the outsiders. The whistle he carried acted as a first alert that someone was in trouble. Hope wondered if he had any news for them. *At least he hasn't used the whistle*, Hope thought morosely. The only time he had used the whistle was to alert the neighborhood when her husband had gone missing.

She hated the whistle.

Forcing a smile to her face, Hope raised a hand in greeting as she stepped into the front yard. "Hi, Marty, how are things?"

Marty nodded. "Hi Hope, kids…"

At forty-five years old, retired for two years, his buzz cut had grown out a bit but he still retained a military posture. Hope admired him for what he did. He had taken over a difficult, almost impossible task, and he never once complained. Marty, along with the team he had put together, made sure that the looting and crime that was rampant in the surrounding counties did not invade the neighborhood. He was thorough and friendly, but she had no doubt that if confronted with a threat he would respond with equal force.

Some level of law still existed, but Marty had told her he didn't put a whole lot of faith in what was out there. Hope remembered his words at the beginning of the collapse. "I don't want to trust the people who are part of an organization linked to the government. We're in this situation because of the government, so why would I have any faith in them?" Although he grudgingly accepted that the government night patrols enforced the recently imposed martial law, he refused to relinquish daytime security and spent his days patrolling the neighborhood. Marty was trained to kill, and Hope knew that in a dangerous situation he would always fire first and ask questions later. She was simultaneously afraid and relieved that he lived near her.

Standing before her, Marty grew silent. Hope knew without having to be told that something was wrong. A sour taste rose in her throat. "Okay, kids, why don't you go in the house and get the fireplace set up for me?"

"I want to stay on lookout," Sandy whined.

Hope hesitated until she saw Marty's slight nod. "Go on in the house, sweetie. I'll be in soon. Maybe after we cook we can play a board game."

"I'll handle lookout for a little while," Marty boomed. At that, Sandy scrambled out of the tree and followed her big brother into the house.

Hope opened her mouth to speak, but the words got caught. *Does he have news? It can't be good, not the way he's looking at me.*

"It's not about your husband. I'm sorry," Marty said.

She knew it was unreasonable, but she couldn't help feeling disappointed. It was probably well past the time that she could expect her husband back, but there was no dislodging the hope from her heart.

"My sources tell me we're about to have another problem," Marty's words were rushed. "I think this one is going to be bad, and there's no telling where it might lead."

"Sources?"

"People I know. We've been communicating on satellite radio."

"Radio?" Hope knew she sounded like an idiot, but she couldn't help it.

"It's the one thing that hasn't gone down. Don't worry, it's from the army and it's secure."

Hope shook her head. Sometimes the bizarre nature of this new world made her feel as if the ground beneath her was no longer solid. "What did your, um, sources tell you?"

Marty looked around discreetly before answering in a quiet voice. "We all know that everything has been shutting down. There's no money, no way to get anywhere, and no real reason to stay if things are bad. Now it's really going to hit the fan."

Hope was confused. "What are you talking about?"

"You know of Eastern State Hospital, right?"

With a sense of dread Hope nodded, uncertain she wanted to hear this.

"Nobody's working. Why go to work when you're not going to get paid?"

"So nobody's there for the patients," Hope said.

Marty nodded. "As of this morning, the patients have all left the building."

Hope swallowed nervously. "But, these are psychiatric patients. Where would they go?"

Marty stared at her with an intensity that was unnerving. "Without medication, who knows what most of those folks are going to do. It's sad, and under normal circumstances I wouldn't be worried about people with mental health issues, but we no longer have normal circumstances. I'd say we're going to have to be prepared for some kind of issue from that group."

Hope shook her head, trying to think clearly. "But Marty—" Hope stopped herself, trying to sort her thoughts before she spoke.

Marty's gaze was direct. "I know what you're thinking, Hope. They're just people, what's the harm, we don't know that they're headed toward us, right?" Hope nodded. "While that is certainly valid, this is still a concern. Plus, we've got other problems we need to discuss. I'm calling a neighborhood meeting tonight at the Warren's house. We've got security issues, and we need to talk about our future."

The constant feeling of dread that had lodged in her stomach tightened. A note of resignation crept into her voice as she asked Marty what time they should be at the meeting.

"Six o'clock sharp. Bring some food; we're going to share what we have. And be ready for some changes, Hope. We've had a security breach on our perimeter and we need to shore up our resources. See you tonight." With a wave he left, no doubt to spread the word about the meeting.

"Mom?"

Hope jumped. Sandy stepped out from behind the dusty, unused car in the driveway. Her eyes were brimming with tears.

"What is it? Are you okay?" Hope went to her and knelt down, wiping the tears from her daughter's face.

"Wh-what did Mr. Conway say? Has he seen Daddy?"

Hope's arms enveloped her daughter. "No, sweetie, he hasn't seen or heard from your father." The question startled Hope. She hadn't even been thinking about the holidays—how could she? What the hell kind of Christmas would this year bring? She had to somehow balance reality with trying to preserve her children's emotional well-being. "Mr. Conway knows lots of people who are watching for him, and if anyone hears anything Mr. Conway will tell us. Right now all we can do is hope for the best."

She stood for a moment with her arms wrapped around her little girl, trying to offer some measure of comfort. Sandy pulled away. "I'm going inside to play."

Hope watched her walk inside the house, wondering how she was going to be able to protect her children. *Sometimes I think it's not even the physical dangers I need to protect them from as much as all the heartache that's coming our way.*

Taking a deep breath, Hope turned her mind to other pressing matters. Tonight's dinner was her first obstacle. With the scarcity of food, community dinners were always easier. As she thought about what she had on hand to bring, she let out a short laugh. "Good thing I used to shop at the superstores. Buying in bulk was not just economical; it's been a lifesaver for meals. Literally."

She still had rice she could cook, and she could add the few tomatoes and wild onions that she had managed to grow. A pinch of salt and that would feed more than a couple of people. After the collapse, everybody's tastes had changed. Not that long ago most people she knew wouldn't touch a meal that wasn't properly seasoned and without meat. Hunger drove people to eat things they might not have thought possible, including dubious combinations of edible plants and flowers.

Or anything they could get their hands on. She couldn't stop the thread of panic that crept into her thoughts. *What will it be like in the long winter months, once our food supply is gone?*

CHAPTER TWO

ALTHOUGH SERIOUS TOPICS WERE TO be discussed at the night's meeting, Hope treated the event as a social occasion. She decided to wear a long black skirt with flat shoes paired with a long-sleeved turquoise silk blouse. Despite the fact that it was November, the weather was still warm. With her long, dark hair pulled back and a hint of makeup to complete the look, Hope felt almost normal. Almost.

For obvious reasons nobody went out anymore; no movies were showing at the cinema and restaurants had all closed down weeks ago. Besides that, there were inherent dangers in going into crowded areas. People were desperate and crime had risen dramatically. Drug addicts needed a fix, people were hungry and thirsty, and the rules of social structure were gone. Safety came first, and safety existed only with known groups of people.

Dusk was falling when the people of the neighborhood gathered at the Warren's house. Marty had told everyone the

Warren's was one of the safer homes in the area, since it sat almost in the center of the other homes and streets. To protect the neighborhood, Marty had convinced people who lived on the perimeter to abandon their homes. Once the perimeter was established, the entry and exit points were always guarded. With the population down to just over one hundred people, it was the best they could do.

When Hope and the kids arrived she was surprised to find that there weren't as many people as she expected. Placing her rice dish on the kitchen counter, Hope turned to Sharon Warren and smiled. "Hey, how are you tonight?"

Sharon nodded. "As good as can be expected, I guess. Looks like there won't be as many people joining us tonight."

"Why not?"

"Marty said that about half the neighbors have decided they didn't like how things were going around here. They think we should make an effort to get more guns and take a stronger stance on our security."

"But Marty is tight on security. He doesn't allow strangers to get through and he's the one that originally came up with the idea to secure the neighborhood. What more do these people think we should be doing?"

Sharon shrugged. "I don't really know what they want, but Ed seems to think that it's about power for them. Maybe they're looking to start their own little fiefdom or something, where they are in complete control."

Hope shuddered. "This whole thing is surreal. People have lost their minds. Anyway, never mind them. We're better off without them."

Sharon raised a glass of water in salute. "You're right, we are better off without them. Who needs to be surrounded by even more lunatics?"

Hope laughed. "So, how's it going here at home? Are you and

Ed getting along okay?"

With a derisive snort, Sharon answered. "Splendidly. Who knew that a national catastrophe could bring us back together? Honestly, Hope, after I found out he was having an affair I thought I could never live with him again. But here I am."

"Here you are," Hope repeated softly. "Sharon, I know this has got to be hard for you, but for what it's worth, I think you're doing the right thing. You put your children and their safety first, and you're all better off here together than scattered around the county with who knows what going on out there."

"You're right, thanks Hope. I'm sorry if I sound selfish, I know that this has got to be difficult for you, too. Have you heard any news about Harlan?"

"No, and with every day that goes by I feel more and more guilty. I should have never let him go out there on his own."

Sharon shook her head. "You didn't know what could happen, none of us knew. It's not your fault."

Hope disagreed. "Both my husband and I should have known better. Neither one of us had any business wandering the streets by ourselves, but for some reason we thought Harlan would be okay out there on his own. He insisted we needed information and he thought he might be able to find us food somewhere. Apparently we were wrong."

Doubt crept into her mind again as it had over the past weeks. Sure, maybe something had happened to Harlan. But she also knew about the rumors. Rumors of him being involved in something shady, rumors of him taking money, rumors of criminal activity. Maybe he really was trying to get back to his home, his family, his life, but the odds were good that the rumors were true. *Nothing I can do about any of this, so I'll continue to push it out of my mind and forget about it. If Harlan makes it back to us then I'll confront him, but until then I can't let the kids know I doubt their father.*

Sharon put an arm around Hope. "Let's hope and pray for the best, okay? In the meantime, come on out in the backyard and enjoy the neighbors. Let's try to have some fun before Marty lays down the new laws for us."

Walking into the backyard, Hope looked around at the neighbors that had gathered. Ruth and Frank, both of them in their early eighties, sat quietly at a wrought iron table on the back deck. Hope knew they both had complicated health problems, but so far they seemed to be holding up just fine. Next to them sat Joan, a single mother of three, content to sit in silence for a few moments while her children swarmed around the large wooden play set. Michael and Corrine Jensen circulated through the crowd, talking to everyone and trying to be upbeat. As grandparents, they used to care for their two toddler grandchildren, but that was no longer the case. She knew they missed their children and grandchildren, but because of what had happened both were wary of venturing out to be with them. Each neighbor had a unique story, and each of them was trying to survive the best they knew how.

Looking across the patio Hope saw Marty staring at her, his blue eyes concerned as he assessed the social situation. With a slight nod at her, he turned to Sharon and said, "I think everyone who wants to be here has arrived. Let's begin."

"Hey, shouldn't we eat first?" Ed called from across the patio.

Marty shook his head. "There will be plenty of time for that after we discuss a couple of things. We're going to need time together to talk, so let me say what I have to say first. We can eat and have further discussion after dinner."

The children drew closer to their parents as a hush settled over the crowd. Marty squared his shoulders and began. "As I have already reported to most of you, we have a situation where the patients at Eastern State Hospital have been released. While this may or may not be a concern for us, we have other security issues that need to be addressed. First, from what I can gather, things in Newberg are rapidly deteriorating. Since it's a more urban environment than here, they don't have the resources we have."

"You mean the wealth of squirrels and rabbits," a voice shouted. Uneasy laughter rippled through the crowd as Marty acknowledged this fact.

"True, they don't have all the furry little creatures that help feed the families in this town. Plus, although troops have been patrolling the streets there is no help for the citizens." Marty hesitated for a moment, glancing at some of the children sitting before him. "Hey kids, why don't you go in the house and start organizing the plates and cups for dinner?" While the younger ones went inside agreeably, some of the older kids stayed to listen. Hope noticed that Jared was one of them.

"Jared," Hope called, "why don't you go help your sister?"

Glaring at his mother, Jared slowly got to his feet and walked toward the house. Hope decided to ignore the fact that he stood just outside the door, waiting to hear what Marty had to say.

Marty noticed, and called out, "You heard your mother, go on in and help your sister. Don't worry, you're really not missing anything. You'll hear all about this and be part of our planning later tonight." Hope nodded her thanks to Marty, watching as Jared quietly slipped inside the house.

Marty turned back to the crowd. "Remember what happened in New Orleans post Katrina? Well, it looks like we've got a situation very similar going on right now, except it's happening in places all over the country."

Ruth called out in a shaky voice, "Marty, what on earth are you talking about?"

He took a breath before continuing. "People can't get their medication, or are starving, or hurt, and the result is that they're dying at a really fast rate. Unfortunately, nobody knows what to do with the bodies in the cities. They have no place to put them.

Dead bodies have been put out in the streets and left there, rats crawling all over them. Of course this is going to create more problems down the line."

Frank, who had difficulty hearing, hollered, "When is this mess all going to get straightened out? We live in the greatest country on earth, what in tarnation is happening around here?"

Ed sounded bitter when he spoke. "Our country got itself into a world of trouble by being in debt. Lots of people saw this coming, but nobody really knew what to do about it. We kept borrowing more and more, and things like plummeting stocks and housing, lack of energy resources and declining credit all made this mess we're in now."

Frank was indignant. "You mean to tell me that because we owe a bunch of foreigners some money that means we ran out of food and fuel? Why don't we just send our troops in and take care of the problem?"

Marty sighed. "Frank, I know it's difficult, but the reasons we are in this mess are not really anything we can change at this point. The whole world is in a big mess. However, we do have some pressing problems that need to be addressed first. I'll stop by your house tomorrow afternoon and we can talk privately about this, okay?"

"Fine. But I still think we need to remember what made this country great and get ourselves back on our feet again."

"You are absolutely right," Marty agreed. "But first we need to figure out how we're going to survive the coming months and years."

A deep silence descended on the crowd as Hope absorbed Marty's words. Some small part of her had held onto the hope that maybe things would get better and go back to the way they were, but as time passed that hope was fading. *This time of year we're usually getting ready for the holidays... I don't think Santa's going to be able to help us now.*

Clearing his throat, Marty continued. "My concern is that there has already been one security breach in the neighborhood. One of the men that we have watching our eastern front entry point allowed persons of unknown origins to cross into our area."

"Foreigners?" Frank yelled.

"No, not foreigners exactly, just people from other areas that were actually looking to rob some of the homes here. They were apprehended during a routine patrol I was on with Ed."

"That whole thing was ridiculous," Sharon sputtered. "What do these people think they're doing, anyway? Nobody has any electricity across the whole country. What good does it do to steal televisions and computers when they can't be used?"

"Most of us have no idea how long this will last," Marty answered quietly. "Looting and robbing is kind of like saving for a rainy day. People are banking on the fact that at some point in the future everything will get back to normal."

"Did ya shoot 'em?" Frank asked. "Cause if ya didn't, then that's too bad. They shoulda been shot."

Marty was clearly trying to suppress a grin. "No, sir, we did not shoot anyone. We simply escorted them out, but we did let them know that an execution was a definite possibility. Hopefully that will stop them from coming back."

"Probably not. Besides, there'll be more," Hope said quietly.

Marty looked at her and nodded. "There will be more."

Corinne, quiet until this point, asked, "Marty, what are you proposing we do now? Get more security? I don't see how that will be possible since we have a number of neighbors that won't even participate in meetings like this one."

"You're right, Corinne. There's a small contingent in this area trying to establish that they are in charge and have begun holding secret meetings to discuss a sort of takeover."

"Can't be too secret if you're tellin' us about it," Frank noted.

"I have sources they are unaware of. But to answer your

question, Corinne, no, I don't think more security is the answer. I see us as having problems on several levels. First and most obvious is the security. As people become more desperate I'm afraid a perimeter breach will mean folks will be in here not just stealing our stuff but maybe even worse. I don't like the idea of fending off violent intruders. But more importantly, we're all aware that we have limited food and water resources. Water is a big problem. We've got rain barrels, but that hasn't yielded much. The creek on the west side of the neighborhood has come in handy for a water source, but we haven't had much rain in the past couple of weeks. If that creek dries up we'll be —"

"Up a creek," Hope finished. "Obviously we can't last long without water, but it's not like we can just lock our houses up and leave."

"That's exactly what we may have to do. I would like to propose that we move everyone to a safer location. My sources say that there is a community further north, up in the Middlesex area, where folks have plenty of food and water and have created a sustainable village. They've actually been living there since before the collapse."

"Sustainable village?" Doubt was evident in Ed's voice. "What, exactly, does that mean?"

"It means they're living in a rural environment and have a greater ability to fend for themselves. There's more room to grow food and less people to cause trouble. The creek that starts in our neighborhood ends up feeding into the river that runs alongside Middlesex, so they have a better water source. Security is tight and I don't think they'll be letting strangers in for much longer. I'd like to propose that we organize ourselves and get on over there before things get much worse here."

"Why will it be better there? I'm not sure we should leave what we know," Ed said.

"It will be better because this is a group that has been living off the grid for some time now. They're used to not depending on outside resources for things like food and water. I've heard a doctor lives there, and that means some form of health care. Plus, they've been an established community for a while."

"No power struggles," Hope said, thinking of the small contingent of people in her neighborhood looking to take over.

"No power struggles," Marty agreed.

"But how are we going to get there when we don't have any gas for the cars?" Joan asked.

"We'll do it the old fashioned way, missy. We'll use our God-given two legs and walk." Frank's tone clearly indicated his disgust.

"That's exactly what we'll do," Marty added. "In fact, I have a plan."

"Wait a minute," Joan interrupted. "Do you mean you want us to leave our homes behind and go live out in the middle of nowhere? You've got to be kidding me. What's going to happen to our houses?"

"What's going to happen to us if we don't?" Hope asked. Leaving her home behind was terrifying on several levels, but Marty was right. They couldn't survive without water. "I can see the truth of what you're saying, Marty, but some may be a little hesitant to leave."

"I'm not forcing anyone to do anything. All I'm saying is it might be a better option for us to get to safer ground. I, for one, am planning on heading out there. If anyone wants to join me, I'll see to it we get there safely. For those of us who choose to go up to Middlesex, well, I can only guess that somehow word will get out to others where we went," Marty answered, looking directly at Hope.

"And you really think we'll be better off up there?"

Marty nodded. "Not a doubt in my mind. Our society has disintegrated, and we're rapidly running out of resources. We need to get to a safe haven. Unfortunately, our little suburban paradise here isn't enough."

Throughout the rest of the evening the neighbors debated and argued the merits of moving. Opinions were strong on both sides, but by the end of the night most people had made some sort of decision for themselves.

As neighbors prepared to leave in groups to go back to their houses, Marty approached Hope. "Well? Staying or going?"

She hesitated briefly. "There's not much choice, is there?" she asked softly. "My first priority is my kids. I need to do everything I can to keep them safe and provide for them. And you're right, you know. Another summer like we had this year and that creek will be bone dry. I thought there'd be more rain this fall, but… We'll go with you."

"It's a good move, Hope. You'll be safer with us."

Hope wanted to believe him, but the week that followed found doubt crowding her heart and mind. What if it was riskier to travel on the roads to another town? What if the sustainable village Marty spoke of refused to take them in? But most importantly, what if Harlan came back and they were gone?

CHAPTER THREE

TWO NIGHTS AFTER THE DINNER meeting, Hope opened her eyes to complete darkness. *Must be about three in the morning*, she thought. *Why am I awake?*

A moment later she heard it. Gutteral shrieks, screams… She shivered, rubbing her arms where goosebumps were raised. *What the hell is that?* Grabbing a baseball bat from the corner by her bed, she crept to her window and peeked outside. She couldn't see anything, but the howls had stopped. Coyote? Could they be that close that she could hear them through a closed window?

Moments later she saw them, dark figures running down the street. People running away. She sank down from the window even though she knew they couldn't see her. *What the hell?* Who were they, and where did they come from?

She crawled into the living room, afraid to stand in case anyone was outside the house. She didn't want to be seen.

Sitting on the floor, she leaned her back against the front door and waited for dawn. She was ready to defend her children with whatever she had. *They'll have to get through me, first.*

* * *

The next day Marty stopped by to tell her that another home on her street had been broken into. Her neighbors, a twenty-something formerly professional couple, were badly beaten and left for dead. The shrieks that she'd heard the night before echoed through her mind. For whatever reason, guards had not been positioned at the entry points to the neighborhood. *We need more protection. Dear God, what if…*

The thought was too unbearable to finish. Her decision to leave was clearly the right one. They couldn't go on like this.

As she sorted through their clothes, deciding what to bring and what to leave behind, Hope thought about what might happen if others came looking to raid the homes in the neighborhood. "Upper middle class suburbia just isn't what it used to be," she thought wryly, placing a sweater on top of the pile of clothes that would be carried with them.

Around twenty-five people decided to make the journey to Middlesex. Each person was assigned to carry a backpack, while wagons, carriages, and strollers were gathered to carry supplies.

"Mommy, how long will it take us to get there?"

Hope paused, welcoming the break her daughter offered. "This is just a guess, but I think it might take us five or six days."

Sandy looked horrified. "We're going to walk for five or six days? Why will it take us so long?" Her face brightened for a moment. "I know, maybe we can run and get there quicker."

Hope smiled. "The place we're going to is about thirty five miles from our house. But remember, we can only go as fast as the slowest person that is with us. We have to stay together as a group, and some people don't have the same amount of energy you have."

Sandy's forehead wrinkled. "So, what you mean is we can only walk as fast as Mrs. Fletcher."

"That's right. We don't want to leave her behind, do we?"

"No, I guess not. But mommy, are you sure daddy will know where to find us? What if he can't find us?"

"It doesn't really matter, Sandy, I've already told you he's not coming back." Jared stood in the doorway, arms crossed in a defensive position.

"Jared, please don't speak to your sister like that. We don't know where your father is, and we don't know what happened to him. For now, let's hope for the best and assume he's doing everything he can to get back. To answer your question, Sandy, your father will know where to find us because I'm leaving messages for him if he comes back. Don't worry; he'll know exactly where we went."

"So, we're like supposed to walk for a week and get to some strange place full of people we don't know who might or might not take us in and then hope that Dad can walk to us after he's been wherever he's been?" Jared snorted. "Right, Mom. That'll work."

Hope stepped in front of Jared. "Now you listen to me, young man. I understand how you're feeling. I'm just as upset as you are about this. But right now we've got each other, and we've got to try to survive as best we can. We're leaving in two days, and I know if your father were here he would tell me it's the right thing to do. Now you'd better figure out a way to change your attitude, and you'd better figure it out quick."

"Or what? You'll take my video games away?" Jared turned and stalked down the hall to his room.

"No, Jared, or you won't be able to hold your heart open." It didn't matter if Jared heard her or not, she knew he wasn't ready to understand what she was saying. Every day that went by broke her heart a little bit more as she watched her children struggle, and she could clearly see their last hope for a better life right now was to go somewhere else. Thank god for Marty, she thought, not for the first time that week. If anyone could get them to safety, she knew Marty could do it. At least, that's what they were all counting on.

Marty's plan for moving everyone was simple. Two days after the break-in at her neighbors they gathered at the Warren's house again, this time ready to move.

"Okay, I need to form a rectangle," Marty called out. "I need all the young, strong men and women on the outside, and children and older folks on the inside. My outside rectangle will receive weapons. You are our line of defense in case of an attack from any of the rogue wackos wandering the streets. I will be at the rear of the formation and will give the order to shoot if necessary. Aim for the heart. If you have to shoot, shoot to kill."

As everybody gathered and formed an orderly rectangle formation, Hope's heart leapt into her throat. Her son, Jared, had placed himself on the outside of the formation.

"Jared, honey, why don't you –"

"No, Mom, I'm part of the first line of defense. I'm young and strong and I know how to shoot." Jared held his head high, and added, "It's what Dad would have wanted."

Hope's heart shattered as memories of Jared, with his newborn head full of peach fuzz, flashed through her mind. He was a part of her, and yet she needed to let him do this. Unable to speak, she simply nodded. Hope took a position on the outside as well, three people behind Jared. *God help the person who tries to hurt my son*, she thought. *I will tear a hole in his throat.*

And so the long walk began, one step at a time. Initially people talked and joked, but as the day wore on and blisters started to form on hands and feet the mood became more somber. There were many stops for bathroom breaks, and the children's complaints grew as the hours dragged by. Ruth and Frank, the most elderly of the group, threw constant apologies out to everyone.

"We are so sorry to hold you all up. If you want to go ahead we'll be okay," Ruth said, shaking her head. "I know I'm the slowest here, and I don't want to be the reason it takes so long."

Murmurs of disagreement rippled through the group. "We're not leaving you behind, Ruth," people told her.

"You can't get rid of us that easily," Ed joked, trying to make light of the situation.

At dusk they stopped, having crossed the bridge and traveled almost seven miles for the day. "We can make our camp behind that strip mall over there," Marty announced, pointing to a deserted area. "After we set the tents up we can eat, then everyone goes to sleep. We need our rest, we've got a long ways to go still. We'll take turns guarding the area, and try to be up at first light to keep moving."

With everyone working together, pitching tents went quickly. A large fire was built and a feast of squirrel and rabbit, courtesy of Marty and Ed, was enjoyed for dinner. "Make sure the fire gets put out quickly," Marty told them. "I don't want that light on any longer than it has to be."

"But it might be nice to sit around a campfire together," Joan complained.

"And it might be nice if we stayed hidden from anyone who might be out there," Marty retorted. With a sniff, Joan hustled her kids into their tent for the evening. Hope was again glad that Marty was in charge. *He's right, we can't take chances.*

Hope was surprised at how tired she was and more than a little grateful that sleep came quickly. Jared and Sandy, thankfully, fell asleep just as soon as they settled into the tent. The one heavy blanket Hope had carried with them served to keep the family warm, and they used sweatshirts as makeshift pillows.

It seemed like only minutes later that Hope was awake, startled out of her sleep. Disoriented in the murky darkness, she lay still, wondering what was out there. Slowly it occurred to her there was a rhythmic tapping on the tent. Sometime during the night a steady rain had begun, making the early dawn hours gray and darker than normal.

I do miss the weather channel, even if they got it wrong most of the time, Hope thought. *Put that on my list of things I used to take for granted.*

The group of campers was slow to rise, as nobody was looking forward to the long, wet walk they faced.

"C'mon, folks, the sooner we get moving the sooner we get to our destination," Marty urged everyone. "We'll be okay, just put one foot in front of another and keep moving. Don't think, just move. Let's go."

After sharing a meager breakfast of potatoes and bitter chicory coffee the group got back on the road. The rain made talk a little more difficult, but there were some who tried to keep everyone's spirits up with their banter.

"I've been meaning to start training for a marathon," Ed joked. "I just didn't know I'd be doing it so soon."

"Hey, Ed, at the rate you can run you'll be training for the Lead Man competition instead of the Iron Man."

"Oh yeah? Maybe we should have a little jousting competition at our next campsite."

The attack happened so quickly there was barely time to react. From behind a storefront on the right a group of strangers lunged at them, faces masked with grime and desperation. Looking into the frenzied eyes of a bearded man as he rushed toward her, Hope knew that these were people that had lost their grip on sanity. Raising her gun she fired off a shot in conjunction with Marty's booming command.

"Fire!"

CHAPTER FOUR

GUNSHOTS MINGLED WITH SCREAMS. HOPE took aim and fired, but her attacker kept coming. She took a step backward, but he was on her, pulling her toward him. Her breath came in short gasps as she kicked and punched, clawing at his face. Grabbing her, he pulled her onto the ground as she struggled against him. Punching and kicking did no good as his weight bore down on her, pinning her to the ground. He raised a knife, and without thinking she tried to roll to her side, struggling to dislodge the man from her body before he killed her. As his arm went back he suddenly fell off of her. Breathing heavily, Hope watched as Marty threw the man to the ground and kicked him in the stomach. Taking aim, Marty prepared to shoot the attacker, but was momentarily distracted by a ghastly scream coming from their group.

One of the neighbors from their group, Hilary, was being dragged off by two men. As she struggled and screamed, one of the crazies, as Hope now thought of them, grabbed Hilary's hair, pulled her head back and kicked her in the gut. Her screams stopped, but they used her as a shield so Marty and the others couldn't shoot. Just as quickly as they'd arrived they were gone, taking Hilary with them.

Hope struggled for her own breath as she watched her neighbor's body being dragged off to a probable death. Crawling to Jared and Sandy, Hope gathered her children into her arms and held them tight.

The sound of sobbing broke out after a moment of silence. Jeff, Hilary's husband, sat on the ground holding his head in his hands. Friends gathered around him.

"Is anyone injured?" Marty asked in a subdued voice. "Ruth, Frank, are you okay?"

Ruth and Frank nodded, silent. Hope sat, stunned and uncertain of what to say to Jeff. He and Hilary had only been married for two years. As successful twenty-somethings, they had their whole lives ahead of them and had planned on living the American dream of children and a dog in suburbia. They had no children and their dog was long gone. The dream had become a nightmare.

"I don't mean to sound harsh, but I think the best thing is for us to get up and keep moving." Marty's voice sounded shaky. "We don't know who those people were or if there are more of them, and I really don't ever want to see them again. They may be off somewhere re-grouping, and I wouldn't be surprised if they plan on coming back."

Jeff looked up at Marty. "But, we can't just let them take her."

Marty hesitated for a moment. "I'm sorry, man, I really am. But I think that for our safety we need to get out of here. I counted more than fifty people in that group, and who knows how many more they have back at their camp. I want to get her, but I'm afraid we're outnumbered. And it looks like they took a lot of our supplies. I'm sorry, Jeff, I really am…" His voice trailed off as he stood, obviously uncomfortable and holding his right arm.

"Marty, are you hurt?" Hope asked. "It looks like you're bleeding."

Marty nodded. "Yeah, my arm got cut. I'm okay, though, it's not a bad wound. I'll wrap it as we keep walking. But we really need to keep walking."

Shaken and wary, the group somehow managed to pick up the few things left on the ground and get moving again. By unspoken consent Jeff was put in the middle of the group, as if they could form a barrier of support that might somehow help him.

Trudging through the muddy street, soaked by the steady rain, adrenaline coursed through Hope. She glanced around nervously, hoping that there wouldn't be another attack, knowing in her heart that this little group could not withstand any more violence that day. Shivering, Hope put her arms around her children as they pushed on, grateful once again that they had been spared.

Marty hid his pain well. He had already soaked two shirts with his blood, with no signs of slowing down.

"Marty, please, let's take cover somewhere so I can wrap your arm properly. We can't afford to have something happen to you now," Hope pleaded with him. *We'll die.* Her unspoken thought hung in the air.

Marty agreed. "I hate stopping, but you're right. Let's find a place to stop."

"Right here is good." Hope had been so focused on Marty that the strange voice caused her to jump. Jared drew his weapon, aiming at the heart of the stranger before them.

"You might want to put that away, son, seeing as how I'm armed too. No point in us both killing each other." The stranger was tall and lean, with several days growth of a beard and shaggy dark hair that reached just below his collar. His direct gaze fell on Marty. "It looks like you folks have seen some trouble."

There was a brief silence before Marty spoke. "We were attacked just a little ways back. Out of nowhere a group of—" Marty struggled to spit out the words, "people came at us. They took one of our group, grabbed her by the hair and took off with her and a bunch of our supplies."

The stranger nodded. "We've been seeing them around here. You're lucky they just took her, it could've been worse. They've done a fair bit of killing, but then again, so have we." He looked the group over and sighed. "You'd better come with me. I assume you're heading out to the farms, right?"

"I don't think that's any of your business," Jared told him defiantly. "Besides, why should we go with you?"

The stranger nodded. "I'm glad to see you've still got some spunk left in you." The smile faded as he added, "What you just went through could have affected you in a whole different way."

"What do you mean, the farms?" Hope asked.

"It's what some folks are calling the village. I call it the farms because several working farms are back there. I've seen a few groups of people heading through here, trying to get up to the farms and find safety."

"Tell us the truth. Is it safe out there?" Sharon asked in a tentative voice.

The stranger nodded. "It's safer than most places. Plus, there's plenty of food and water for an entire village. My wife and I, we've been trying to help folks get through here safely. There's a whole group of people, they're just plain crazy. I don't know where they came from, but you've seen what they can do. We try to act as a sort of safe haven to help you get where you need to go."

"Like a stop on the underground railroad," Sandy piped in.

For the first time, the stranger smiled. "Exactly. Like a stop on the underground railroad. If you follow me I'll take you back to our house. My wife can help you with that wound," he nodded at

Marty, "and you can rest a while. You'll be safe with us, and I can draw you a map with a better route to the farms."

Seconds ticked by as the rain drizzled down. Hope held her breath and looked to Marty. After a moment he gave a brief nod, indicating they should follow the stranger.

It took them almost fifteen minutes to trek to the man's house. During this time they learned his name was Ellis and his wife's name was Shawna. Ellis told the group of the many people that had come through and of his struggles to help them. "Shawna and I, we see it as our responsibility to make this a better place. Once everything collapsed we figured it would get bad, and we were right. We've been stockpiling supplies for years now, waiting for this to happen."

Hope and Marty exchanged a glance. They had heard of people like this, people who were prepared for the eventuality of a complete economic and social collapse. For the first time ever, Hope was thankful they existed.

"You can all spend the night in the house. We'll spread you out in the bedrooms and living room, or wherever there's space. Shawna is probably cooking right now since I told her I was going out on patrol to see if there were any stragglers." He glanced over at Marty. "That's what I call folks who come through here looking for a better place, stragglers. Everyone seems to sort of stumble their way in."

Soon they were at Ellis's home, a two story white clapboard farmhouse beginning to show signs of weathering. A wraparound porch held several rockers, and a cloud of smoke rose from the chimney.

Hope felt like she had come home.

Ellis ushered everyone inside and introductions were made. His wife, Shawna, seemed pleased to meet them. "I'm glad Ellis found you," she told Hope quietly. "It's terrible what's happening out there, and we've been trying to help any way we can."

"Shawna made enough food for everyone," Ellis announced. "In the meantime, feel free to use the bathrooms and get cleaned up."

There was a moment of stunned silence before anyone spoke. "Bathrooms?" Jared squeaked. "But how…"

Ellis smiled at the boy. "Out here we've got well water and what you might call alternative energy. Shawna and I have lived off the grid for quite a while now. We didn't want to rely on the big energy companies for anything."

"What do you mean, off the grid?" Joan asked, her face wrinkled in confusion.

"It means we don't have heating and electricity the way most people do," Shawna explained. "We have a combination of solar, wind and bio-energy sources that provide us with everything we need."

"You mean you have running water?" Ed asked, incredulous.

"Yes, as well as heat and hot water." Pride was evident in Ellis's voice.

Tears welled up in Hope's eyes, and she had to blink them away. "I think our first order of business is to get Marty cleaned up. He's still bleeding."

Shawna reached out to touch Marty's arm. "Come with me and I'll take care of that. I have a stockpile of medicinal supplies that we can use."

Of course they have medicinal supplies, Hope thought, wondering if she was on the verge of hysteria. *Why wouldn't they?*

"Mom," Jared interrupted Hope's thoughts. "Are you okay? You look kind of weird."

"I'll be fine," Hope reassured him. "I'm overwhelmed, that's all. I feel like we've won the lottery."

"Your timing is perfect," Ellis said, coming into the room. "Do you know what today is?"

"Our lucky day?" Sandy said.

Ellis smiled. "I think it's a lucky day for all of us, because we get to celebrate Thanksgiving together. We have a lot to be thankful for, don't you think?"

"Today is Thanksgiving?" Sandy's eyes were huge.

How had she forgotten the date? And were they lucky? Hope's first thought was No, life sucks, but she knew he was right. Her kids were safe and they were with her. Her husband was gone, but maybe he had reasons for not coming back. She had no control over him. Maybe she was better off without him, anyway. Maybe this new world gave them all a chance to start over. After all, the pioneers that came to this country had survived—flourished, even. She would too.

Later that day, with the twenty-four of them welcomed into the farmhouse, they gathered throughout the rooms for dinner. Some sat at the dining room table, others in the kitchen, living room and family room. Venison and fresh vegetables were passed around, and for the first time in months Hope's edge of anxiety eased.

After dinner, the core group gathered in the kitchen to discuss their next step.

"I'm going to draw you a map," Ellis told Marty. "If you follow this trail you'll be much safer. There are others along the way who will look out for you, too. You may not see them but you'll be much better protected than you would be on the main road."

Marty shook his head. "To be honest with you, I wasn't sure what would be better, but I thought that traveling the main road would be safer than hiking through the woods."

Ellis nodded. "I know, it's not an easy call to make. But around here the lunatics that attacked you seem to hang around the main route. I think they may be hiding out in empty storefronts."

"How will we know when we get there?" Sandy asked. "Is there a sign?"

Shawna gave the little girl a hug. "Don't worry, honey, I promise you'll know when you get there. I don't think you've ever seen anything like this before."

Again, Hope's eyes filled with tears. "Thank you. I don't know what else to say, except thank you."

"You're welcome."

CHAPTER FIVE

THE FOLLOWING DAY DAWNED CRISP and clear. "I hate walking through the rain," Jared muttered, looking out the window. "I hope this weather lasts at least until we get there."

Setting off on their journey again, Hope and Marty paused in front of the farmhouse. "I know we've all said it already, but thanks. Your kindness will be remembered," Marty told the couple.

"It's what we do," Shawna replied. "Just take care of yourself, and remember to take the rest of those pills I gave you to keep an infection from getting into your arm. I wish you could stay, but we don't have the room. You'll find plenty of space for you at the village."

"I think we need to go now," Joan interrupted. "We've got a long walk, and I am not looking forward to tics and mosquitoes."

Hope and Marty looked at each other, trying not to laugh. Joan seemed to have been able to find plenty to complain about, and for some reason both Hope and Marty had started to find it amusing.

"What's so funny?" Joan demanded.

"Nothing, you're right, let's get going," Marty said, obviously struggling to keep a straight face. He turned back to Ellis. "Are you sure it's okay to leave Jeff with you?"

Ellis nodded. "I think it's best. He's not doing so well, and who can blame him after what he saw happen to his wife. Everyone handles things differently, and we'll make sure he has a quiet place to rest for a while and try to pull himself together. If he decides to join you, I'll see to it that he gets there."

There wasn't much choice, Hope realized as she listened to the exchange. Jeff had lapsed into silence, unable and unwilling to communicate with anyone after Hilary was dragged off to a horrible fate. For the most part he sat and stared into space, lost in a world of his own. She hoped that he would someday be able to accept that there wasn't anything they could do, but for now he needed to rest.

With waves and a few more hugs, the group set off. Looking at the map, Marty announced, "I think this route may actually be a little bit shorter. Hopefully we'll be there in a few days."

The next three days followed the same routine. Rising at dawn, they ate breakfast and set off on the designated path. When the sun was high overhead they stopped for a quick lunch, and set off again until dusk. The night camps were quickly set up while dinner was prepared. Ellis and Shawna had given the group a supply of extra food and water, making meals more enjoyable and less worrisome.

Occasionally Hope glanced at the woods around her, feeling a stir at the back of her neck as if she were being watched. "I feel it too," Marty told her on the second day. "Just keep moving. Ellis said others are watching out for us. If they mean us harm they'll make themselves known."

But they had no more incidents like the one they had on the main road. Toward the end of the third day the group struggled up a steep hill, carrying an exhausted Ruth and assisting Frank through the terrain. The clearing at the top allowed them to see for miles.

Silence filled the air as the group took in the sight before them. Finally, Jared asked in a cracked voice, "What is that?"

"I believe that is the village," Marty answered quietly.

"I know, but what am I looking at?"

In the valley below sat a cluster of twelve homes, some with smoke rising from the chimneys. Hope counted three barns and what looked like several more storage sheds. Horses and cows were in the fields farthest from the homes.

"It looks like they've built a wall," Hope told her son. "They must have gathered anything they could and built a wall to keep everyone safe."

It was a bizarre combination of objects that circled the tiny village, including hand piled stones, fencing materials, sandbags and what looked to be piles of old furniture.

"I'll bet it's very safe in there," Sharon added.

"Is that where we're going to live?" Sandy asked.

"That's the place," Jared said. "Looks like we'll be okay in there."

"Is that where we're going to have Christmas?" Sandy said.

"How can you be thinking about Christmas?" Jared said.

"How could I not?" Sandy countered. "We just had Thanksgiving, and everyone knows Christmas is next."

Hope laughed. "Yes, that is where we're going to have Christmas."

"It won't be the same," Marty said. "But it will be good. We'll make it good."

"We're together, so it will be wonderful. It will just be a different kind of Christmas," Hope said. "Now let's go see if we can find a way into our new home."

Lucky
Christmas

CHAPTER ONE

IT WAS ONE-THIRTY A.M., well past the time to go home. Kylie took a deep breath and leaned over to put her cell phone back in her bag. The remaining convenience store coffee she was holding had grown cold and a headache was forming behind her eyes from the strain of the evening. The only problem was now that it was time to go, she had to tell him. She still had not been able to form the words that needed to be said.

The radio in the car crackled to life. Kylie wondered how anyone could possibly understand the dispatchers. To her, it sounded like nothing but static with lots of incoherent words. Glancing at Nick sitting in the driver's seat, her heart sank. She could tell from the look on his face, not to mention the way he peeled out of the parking lot, she was not going home yet.

"What's going on?" Maybe she didn't want to know.

"Shots fired." Kylie waited for him to elaborate, knowing he wouldn't. Unfailingly polite and not bad to look at, Nick was definitely a man of few words. Or maybe he just didn't want to talk to her.

Shrinking into her seat, she tried not to think of what that phrase meant. Despite the clean, suburban persona of Yorktown, images of gangsters with guns floated through her head. *That kind of thing doesn't happen here, does it?* Unlikely as the possibility was, she didn't want to die from a gunshot wound. *And I don't want to die before Christmas.*

After flipping the siren on, Nick pulled out a cell phone and began barking rapid fire questions to the person on the other end. Removing his remaining hand from the steering wheel, he used his right knee to steer the car as he leaned forward to punch an address into the GPS attached to the windshield. Wherever they were going, it was faster to get there by taking the highway. Watching the speedometer needle climb to ninety, Kylie closed her eyes and held tight to her paper coffee cup. *Please, let there be no ice on the highway… please…*

Kylie dared to open her eyes only when the car slowed. They had entered an industrial area, a part of town she didn't even know existed. Maybe her timing sucked, but if they were going to get shot, she wanted him to know.

"Nick, I have to tell you something."

"C'mon, I know you're here somewhere… they always try to hide, but this time I'm going to catch the little—gotcha!" Slamming on the brakes, he threw the police car into park and opened his door. Shooting a stern look over his shoulder, Nick barked one command. "Stay in the car."

That's pretty much when it all fell apart.

CHAPTER TWO

NICK COULD BARELY FEEL THE ice pack he held on the growing lump on his head. Anger always made him hot, so it was a wonder the ice wasn't immediately turning into water. He shifted on the plastic chair, trying to get comfortable. He had a feeling the captain had ordered these chairs specifically to keep his men off balance.

At the moment, the captain was sitting across from him, leaning forward with his hands on his desk. At least his face wasn't red, and he was only glaring a little. Nick knew when the captain's face got red he was in real trouble.

"Well, deputy, can you tell me what happened out there last night?"

"Yes, sir. I was doing a ride along with a civilian—"

"Kylie," the captain said. "The woman assigned to you."

"Yes sir, Kylie. At the end of my shift I got a call for shots fired in the upper part of the county. I radioed in and responded.

When we got there, I told her to stay in the car. I circled around to try to find the perpetrator, and the next thing I know the officer needs help alarm went off and then deputies from all over swarmed in."

The captain looked stern, but Nick wondered if he was really angry. Usually officers who worked with the captain always knew when they were in trouble by the look on his face. Today, though, annoyance did not reach his eyes. "Did you tell her not to touch that particular button in the vehicle?"

"I told her, I swear I told her, but she must not have been listening, because for some reason she decided to push the red button."

The captain cleared his throat. "I believe she said that she thought you were in danger, deputy."

Nick was confused. How could she have thought he was in any kind of danger? As soon as he realized he had stumbled into a group of residents setting off fireworks, he issued a warning and left. Everybody had been very polite to him. It wasn't until later that morning he learned he had walked into the middle of an undercover operation, but that had not put him in any danger. It had, however, exposed him to ridicule from the detectives he worked with.

The captain, looking stern again, interrupted Nick's thoughts. "Why doesn't your siren work anymore?"

Nick wasn't sure how to answer. He didn't want to get Kylie in trouble, but he wasn't going to take the heat for this one. Trying to sidestep the issue, he said, "I think some coffee might have gotten spilled in the car, sir."

"Coffee."

"Yes, sir."

"And tell me one more thing, deputy."

Nick would answer this question and maybe hopefully get to go home. He was exhausted, and not only from lack of sleep.

That Kylie woman had a way of wearing him out.

"Sir?"

"How did you get a black eye last night?"

Nick swallowed. He had been expecting this and knew he had to answer as truthfully as possible. Hopefully nobody else would find out about this. He didn't want his co-workers to know what had happened.

"I walked into a door, sir. Kylie opened the car door as I was walking over to the car, and it caught me on the side of the head, near my eye."

This time the captain could not stop the grin that spread across his face. "That'll be all, deputy. You better keep that ice pack on your head. And you should go out in the hall and talk to Kylie, she's waiting for you."

Nick couldn't stop the groan that escaped. "What does she want?"

The captain stopped smiling and looked at Nick with something akin to concern. "I think you should give her a chance, she's got something interesting to tell you." Staring for another moment, he added, "I didn't notice it before, but you have the same eyes."

Nick had no idea what the captain was talking about. All he wanted was to get home and sleep. The late night shifts left him exhausted. Saying goodbye, he strode into the hallway to find Kylie sitting in a chair, waiting for him. Without censoring himself, he cut into her. "What the hell were you thinking?"

"You shouldn't clench your jaw like that; it'll give you a headache."

Nick suppressed his urge to yell, realizing it wouldn't do any good. The woman had seemed nice enough at the beginning of the night, but she was quickly proving herself to be the biggest pain in the you-know-what he had ever met. There was a reason most of the deputies didn't like having civilians riding in their cars, but once in a while it had to be done. Twice yearly the department taught a class called the Citizen's Academy, where every week students learned about all facets of law enforcement. Part of the class included riding with a deputy to get a better perspective of the job. For some reason, this woman, Kylie what's-her-name, whom he had never met or seen or even knew existed, had requested him specifically for her ride along.

Lucky him. Maybe this was his early Christmas present.

Rubbing a hand over a day's worth of stubble, Nick took a deep breath. "Okay, I'll ask this once, as nicely as I can. What was the one thing I told you not to do?"

Kylie hung her head, allowing her long auburn hair to cover her face. She didn't say anything for a moment.

Nick cupped his hand around his ear. "I'm sorry, I can't hear you. I know you know the answer to this: the one thing you were not supposed to do…"

She didn't look up. "Don't touch the button," she mumbled.

"Right," he answered in a falsely bright voice. "Don't touch the button. And what did you do?"

Snapping her head up, she glared at him for the first time. "I—"

"Touched the button," he finished for her.

"I thought you were—"

Pointing his finger in her face, he spoke over her. "Not only did you set off an alarm that caused every law enforcement agent in three counties to high tail it over to us, you also managed to disable the siren on the vehicle as well as give me a black eye. I had to explain all that to my captain just now."

They glared at each other for a moment until Kylie looked away. She spoke with an obvious effort. "I was trying to help. I thought those guys were going to attack you, how was I supposed to know they were setting off fireworks? And it wasn't my fault the coffee spilled on the console. Those things shouldn't be able to short out as easy as that, you know. Someone should look into upgrading the equipment."

Nick sighed, running his hand through his already tousled dark hair. He knew she hadn't meant any harm, but what was it they said about the road to hell? "Yeah, and I know you didn't mean to whack me in the face with the car door, it just happened, right?"

"You don't have to be so mean to me."

As her eyes filled with tears Nick purposely hardened his heart. She was like a walking Hallmark movie, an obnoxious Christmas one. It was obvious she wanted something from him, but he wasn't about to let her use histrionics to get it. Towering over her, knowing she was uncomfortable in that stupid plastic chair, he used a deliberately neutral voice. "So, what was it you wanted to tell me?"

For the second time that morning, Kylie glared at him. "You know what? I don't think I want to talk to you right now. You haven't been very nice to me, and all I was trying to do was help. I think I'll let your captain tell you all about it."

Nick straightened. He really did not have time for this. "He told me to talk to you, and he said we have the same eyes. I'm only going to ask you one more time. What's going on?"

Kylie stood, knocking her chair over in the process. "We're here because I know what I did last night I probably shouldn't have done, and I'm sorry there was such a fuss over one little button. I had to explain that to them so *you* wouldn't get into trouble. But in the process of explaining myself, I also told your captain some other things."

"What kind of things?" Nick said. *Was she always this evasive? Why couldn't she just answer a simple damn question?*

"Things about our father."

Realization was slow for Nick. Her words jostled around in his head, not really making sense. It took him a full minute to process what she said, and during that time numbness crawled through him.

"What do you mean, our father? Exactly who are you talking

about?" Because there was no way this bubbly, energetic woman had a father anything like his.

She straightened her shoulders and wiped away her tears. "Your captain has my phone number if you decide to contact me."

Spinning to leave, she tripped on the heel of her boot. Nick grabbed her arm to stop her fall. *This girl is going to hurt herself one of these days.* He couldn't help but wonder at the angry look she shot him as she wrenched her arm away. It wasn't his fault she created so much havoc wherever she went.

CHAPTER THREE

DECEMBER IN VIRGINIA WAS USUALLY cold, but that morning it cut through Kylie more than usual. She shivered, pulled her coat closer around her, and hurried to her car. Things had not gone the way she'd expected. Nick was mean. None of what happened was her fault. Trying to protect someone should be applauded, not condemned.

She stopped at the door to her car, patting her pockets. *Where did I put my keys? Did I lose them?* She dug through her purse, finally finding them. Shivering, freezing cold, she grabbed the keys from the bottom of her bag and yanked them out, only to have them fly out of her hands and skitter under the car.

This keeps getting better. Get the darn keys, get in your car, go home, and go to bed. Everything will be go away then. She bent and could see them just within her reach. On her hands and knees now, she stretched her arm toward the keys. Feet appeared on the other side of her vehicle. *This does not look good.* Her butt was in the air and her face was smashed against the underside of the car door as she tried to reach the keys. She couldn't help that she heard the conversation happening, or that they didn't realize she was right there.

"Glad it wasn't more serious," the first voice said. "But I heard he got it pretty good in the face."

Kylie cringed, knowing who they were talking about.

"Yeah, but at least putting that ice pack on his injury will give him something to focus on over the holidays," a second voice said.

"Don't be mean. I like him, he's just a loner, that's all."

"He works all the time," the second voice said. Kylie had dropped down to her stomach and could see two pairs of feet standing on the other side of her car. The voice continued. "I know he doesn't have any family, but it's not right that he's always here."

"Maybe he likes it that way," the first voice said.

Yeah, maybe he likes it that way. But Kylie knew better.

"I've got to go. The wife is expecting me to watch the kids while she finishes Christmas shopping."

"Good luck with that. This time of year they are all worked up."

"Yeah. Merry Christmas!"

Kylie stayed on the ground, waiting for them to go away. When the sound of the departing cars finally faded, she got up, unlocked her door, and climbed into her driver's seat. Leaning back, she closed her eyes and tried to hold back tears. That conversation changed everything. She knew what she had to do now, but ultimately it would be up to Nick. She couldn't force him into anything, but she sure could try.

CHAPTER FOUR

NICK WAS GRATEFUL FOR THE cover of the night. With the combination of clouds and new moon it was easy to blend with the darkness. The crisp, cold air soothed his tangled nerves. Standing by the tree in the front yard, he could easily see into the front living room where the family had gathered.

They looked happy enough, but his father's words echoed through his mind. "Just cuz they're smilin' don't mean they're happy. Everybody's after something, boy." As if the ghost were by his side, Nick could practically hear him. "What do you want from these people, anyway? More heartache? Stupid kid."

Bitterness rose in his throat as he watched Kylie hug a woman of about sixty, presumably her mother. Memories of his own mother's less than maternal slaps and punches reminded him that not everyone was as fortunate as Kylie. Not everyone got the good home. *Merry freakin' Christmas. I'll bet it's just perfect in there.*

Lost in his thoughts, Nick was startled by the sound of the front door opening. "Nick, are you out there?"

How did she know? She must be some kind of witch. He hesitated, then sighed and stepped forward. He'd better talk to her before she did something calamitous and caused a scene.

"I'm here."

Unbelievably, she smiled at him, radiant. "I knew you'd come."

"How did you know I was already here?"

She gave a half shrug, looking somewhat embarrassed. "You're a cop—I mean, deputy. I figured you'd want to scope the place out before you came in to meet us. Besides, it's Christmas. We're family. It all makes sense."

Actually it didn't, but he wasn't going to argue that point with her. He was defiant. "Just because you left me a message didn't mean I would come. I never called you back to let you know I would be here."

Kylie gazed at him thoughtfully. "Of course you would be here. You're my big brother, aren't you?"

A wave of guilt washed through him. "Half brother," Nick corrected.

Kylie waved a hand at him. "Half, schmalf, who cares how much it is. The point is, I always figured that if I had a brother he would be a great friend and protect me and be lots of fun to hang out with. He could walk me to school and beat up boys that tried to date me. I used to think about that when I was a girl."

Nick was puzzled. "I thought you just found out about me."

"I did. Mom only told me last month she had heard that my, I mean our, father had another child. It's been a long time since they've seen each other, you know."

Nick nodded. "Since the day you were born, right?"

Kylie sucked in her breath. "Did you know about me?"

"No, but I knew about our father." He was not the nicest human being, but he was all Nick had growing up. A half-memory floated by of another Christmas when he was about seven years old. Nick had woken up Christmas morning knowing that what he'd really wanted was not going to be under the tree. A sober father, a bigger family. Those things were just not going to happen in his little world. As he got older, he'd heard the rumors about the other family, the whispers about his father. If he was to be honest with himself, which he probably should right about now, he'd always known a day like this would come.

She looked off into the distance. "I wish we had grown up together, but I can't change that. I would like for you to get to know us, though. You've got nieces and a nephew, and my mother really wants to meet you."

Nick's throat closed, surprising him. Why should he care if some woman wanted to meet him? *Because she's the mother you never knew.* He cleared his throat before speaking. "I'm not very good at family stuff, you know."

"You don't have to be good at family stuff, you just have to care."

Nick was frustrated. It was obvious that Kylie didn't understand where he had come from, what his family life was like growing up. She was one of the lucky kids who got tucked in at night and had bedtime stories read to her. He was lucky just to have a roof over his head. At least that's what his old man told him.

"Mom told me all about him." Kylie's voice was soft in the night. This time it was Nick's turn to look into the darkness.

"Yeah, well, I'm sure it was the same old story, his father was probably a jerk to him, too."

"Is that why you don't have any of your own kids?"

His own laugh sounded harsh in his ears. "No, I've just never really met the right woman. But you're probably right, I don't think I'm exactly father material."

Kylie shook her head. "That's not what I meant and you know it. Come on, you're just trying to delay all this. Come in the house and meet everyone. For heaven's sake, it's Christmas. Have a little holiday spirit."

Nick looked into the house again, which was more of a home than he'd ever known. The Christmas tree lights were flashing, and people were moving back and forth, talking and laughing. Maybe it would be okay to go in and meet them all, just this once. He looked down at Kylie, bouncing on the balls of her feet, excited for him to be there, and sighed.

"Fine, let's go in. But do me a favor, okay?"

Kylie smiled. "Sure, brother, what is it?"

He knew he was asking the impossible, but he had to try. "Can you try to not get us into any more trouble for a while?"

Kylie's smile faded as doubt crossed her face. "I don't mean for bad stuff to happen…"

"It just does," he finished for her. "For my sake, try. It will make my job as your big brother a whole lot easier." He smiled at her to try to take the sting out of the words, but he was serious. That girl knew how to create havoc wherever she went. "All right, I'm ready." He knew his life had changed the moment Kylie found him, and he knew her persistence would not allow him to be left alone. Ready or not, he was about to get a new family.

Walking behind her, Nick was so lost in thought he didn't realize Kylie had stopped walking until it was almost too late. Trying not to plow into her, he lurched backward, lost his balance and fell. Unaware that he had fallen, Kylie turned and said, "Oh, there's one more thing I wanted to tell you."

Nick looked up from the ground. "What?"

"What are you doing on the ground?"

Rising, he slowly brushed himself off. "Nothing. What did you want to tell me?"

"I got a new job!"

Nick froze, the hairs on the back of his neck tingling. He had that feeling he always got right before something big happened, usually something that involved people getting shot or car doors slamming into his face.

He almost didn't want to ask. "What's the job?"

The glow on her face made his heart sink even further. "I got a job with the sheriff's department. I'm going to be the public relations person. Isn't that great? We're going to be working together!"

Nick smiled weakly. It was the best he could do, considering the effect he knew she would have on the department.

"Great," he echoed. "Isn't that… lucky. For you, I mean."

"Nick, I just know it's going to be a wonderful New Year!"

About the Author

Narielle Living is a freelance writer based out of the Hampton Roads area of Virginia. In addition, she is the editor for the Williamsburg magazine Next Door Neighbors. Her mysteries include *Signs of the South, Revenge of the Past,* and *Madness in Brewster Square.* Her fiction also appears in numerous anthologies. She edits both fiction and nonfiction and loves helping other writers achieve their goals. Narielle is currently working on the next books in the Brewster Square series as well as other fun writing projects.

For information about her books or workshops, visit www.narielleliving.com or find her on Facebook, Instagram and Twitter.